LALLIA

ARROW BOOKS

Arrow Books Ltd
3 Fitzroy Square, London W1

An imprint of the Hutchinson Publishing Group

London Melbourne Sydney Auckland
Wellington Johannesburg and agencies
throughout the world

First published 1971
Arrow edition 1977
© E. C. Tubb 1971

Made and printed in Great Britain
by The Anchor Press Ltd
Tiptree, Essex

ISBN 0 09 914050 0

I

ON AARN A man was murdered and Dumarest watched him die.

It was a thing quickly done in a place close to the landing field: a bright tavern of gleaming comfort just beyond the main gate of the high perimeter fence, a cultured place of softness and gentle lighting snugly set on a cultured world. The raw violence was all the more unexpected because of that.

Dumarest saw it all as he stood with his back to a living mural in which naked women swam in an emerald sea and sported with slimed beasts of obscene proportions. Before him, scattered over soft carpets, the customers of the tavern lounged in chairs or stood at the long bar of luminescent wood. An assorted crowd of crewmen and officers, field personnel, traders, and transients. Bright among them was the gaudy finery of pleasure girls, flaunting their charms. Soft music susurrated from the carved ceiling and perfumed smoke stained the air.

Against the softness and luxury the killer looked like a skull at a feast: tall, horribly emaciated, eyes smoldering in the blotched skin of his face. He was a mutant with mottled hair and hands grotesquely large, a sport from some frontier world. He crossed to the long bar, snatched up a bottle of heavy glass and, without hesitation, smashed it on the back of his unsuspecting victim's head. Half-stunned, dazed, the man turned—and received the splintered shards in face and throat.

"Damn you!" The mutant dropped the stained weapon as he spat at the dying man. "Remember me? I swore I'd get you and I have. It's taken years but I did it. You hear me? I did it! I got you, you stinking bastard! Now roast in hell!"

A woman screamed and men came from the shadows to grasp the killer. Dumarest took two long strides towards the door then paused, thinking. The tavern was close to the field, police could not be far away and it was possible that he had already been noticed. To leave now would be to invite suspicion with the resultant interrogation and interminable delay. He regained his position before the mural as officers poured into the tavern. On Aarn the police were highly efficient, and they moved quickly about the tavern as they quested for witnesses. Not surprisingly they discovered them hard to find.

"You there!" The officer was middle-aged, his face hard beneath the rim of his helmet. His uniform was impeccable and the leather of his boots, belt, and laser holster shone with a mirror-finish. "Did you see what happened?"

"Sorry, no," said Dumarest.

"You too?" The officer echoed his disgust. "Over fifty people in the place and no one saw what happened." He glanced over his shoulder towards the scene of the crime. "If you were standing here how could you avoid not seeing? You've a perfect view."

"I wasn't looking that way," explained Dumarest. "I was studying this." He pointed at the mural. "All I heard was some shouting. When I turned the sport was standing over something on the floor. What happened? Did he hurt someone?"

"You could say that," said the officer dryly. "He killed a man with a bottle." He stared curiously at Dumarest, eyes narrowing as he took in the gray plastic finish of pants, knee-boots, and tunic. The tunic was long-sleeved, falling to mid-thigh and fastened high and snug around the throat. It was unusual wear for a city dweller of Aarn. "Are you a resident?"

"No, a traveler. I came here to arrange an outward passage."

"Why not go to the field office?" The officer didn't wait for an answer. "Never mind. I suppose a tavern is the best place to do business if you can afford it. Your papers?"

Dumarest handed over the identification slip given to him when he had landed. The officer checked the photographic likeness and physical details incorporated in the plastic. He softened a little as he saw the credit rating.

"Earl Dumarest," he mused. "Planet of origin: Earth." He raised his eyebrows. "An odd name for a world. I don't think I've ever heard it before. Is it far?"

"A long way from here," said Dumarest flatly.

"It must be. Why did you come to Aarn?"

"To work. To look around." Dumarest smiled. "But main-

6

ly to visit your museum. It is something rather exceptional."

He had struck the right note by his appeal to planetary pride. The officer relaxed as he handed back the identification.

"We're rather proud of it," he admitted and then added, casually, "my son has a position there. In the ancient artifact division, with special reference to Aarn's early history. Did you know that once the planet held an intelligent race of sea creatures? They must have been amphibious and there is evidence they used fire and tools of stone."

"I didn't," said Dumarest. "Not before I visited your museum, that is. Tell me, is your son a tall, well-built youngster with thick curly hair? About twenty-five, with vivid blue eyes?" The officer had blue eyes and the hair on the backs of his hands was thick and curled. "If so I may have met him. A person like that was most helpful to me in my investigations."

"I doubt if that was Hercho," said the officer quickly. "He works in the laboratories. Reconstruction and radio-active dating."

"Specialized work," said Dumarest. "It's a pretty important position for a young man to hold. You must be very proud of him."

"He's done well enough for himself." The officer glanced to where two men carried a stretcher towards the dead man. "May I ask what your own particular subject of interest at the museum might be?"

"Navigational charts and tables," said Dumarest easily. "Really old ones. The type which were in use before the Center-oriented charts we have now. I didn't find any."

"I'm not surprised. We have data from over a hundred thousand habitable worlds and ten times that many items on display, but there has to be a limit. And perhaps you were looking for something which doesn't exist. Are you sure there are such tables?"

"I think so," said Dumarest. "I hope so."

"Well," said the officer politely, "there's no harm in hoping." He turned to move away then halted as Dumarest touched his arm. "What is it?"

"A matter of curiosity," said Dumarest. He nodded to where the attendants carried a sheeted figure towards the door of the tavern. "That man. Who was he?"

"The victim?" The officer shrugged. "No one special. Just a handler from one of the ships."

"The *Starbinder?*"

"The *Moray*. Captain Sheyan's vessel. His name was Elgart. Did you know him?"

"No. I was simply curious."

Dumarest turned to stare at the mural as the dead man
was carried away.

The *Moray* was a small ship, battered, old, standing to
one side of the busy field as if ashamed of associating with
her sister vessels. Her captain matched his command. Ber-
nard Sheyan was small. A ruff of white hair showed beneath his uniform cap. His face, beneath the visor, was
seamed and scored with vicissitude and time. He leaned
back in his chair and stared up at Dumarest over the wide
expanse of his desk.

"You wanted to see me," he snapped curtly. For such a
small man his voice was startlingly deep. "Why?"

"I want a job."

"Forget it. I've a full complement."

"No," said Dumarest flatly. "You haven't. You're short a
handler. A bit of Elgart's past caught up with him and he's
dead."

Sheyan narrowed his eyes. "This past you're talking
about," he said softly. "You?"

"No. I just saw it happen. My guess is that Elgart was
rotten. That he got his kicks from letting those riding Low
wake without the benefit of drugs. One of them finally
caught up with him." Dumarest's eyes were bleak. "If I'm
right, he asked for all he got. The only thing is that he got it
too easily. A man like that should be given a double dose of
his own medicine."

To wake, rising through layers of ebon chill to light and
the stimulating warmth of the eddy currents . . . the scream-
ing agony of returning circulation without the aid of drugs
to numb the pain so that throat and lungs grew raw with
the violence of shrieking torment.

Sheyan said quietly, "You've traveled Low?"

"Yes."

"Often?"

Dumarest nodded, thinking of a skein of barely remembered journeys when he'd traveled doped and frozen and
90 percent dead. Riding in the bleak cold section in caskets
meant for the transport of livestock, risking the 15 percent
death rate for the sake of cheap travel. Risking, too, the

possibility of a sadistic handler who reveled in the sight and sound of anguish.

"So Elgart's dead," mused Sheyan. "You could be right in what you assume, but he didn't play his tricks with me. Even so, he came from one of the big ships and a man doesn't do that without reason. You want his job?"

"Yes."

"Why?"

"I want to leave Aarn," said Dumarest. "Working a passage is better than traveling Low."

Anything, thought Sheyan, was better than traveling Low; but Aarn was a busy world and a hard worker would have little trouble in gaining the cost of a High passage.

He leaned further back in his chair, shrewd eyes studying the figure standing before him. The man was honest, that he liked, and he was an opportunist—few would have acted so quickly to fill a dead man's shoes. He looked at the clothing, at the spot above the right boot where the plastic caught the light with an extra gleam. The hilt of a blade would have caused such a burnishing and it was almost certain that the knife was now tucked safely out of sight beneath the tunic.

His eyes lifted higher, lingering on the hard planes and hollows of the face, the tight, almost cruel set of the mouth. It was the face of a man who had early learned to live without the protection of house, guild, or combine. The face of a loner, of a man, perhaps, who had good reason for wanting a quick passage away from the planet. But that was not his concern.

"You have had experience?"

"Yes," said Dumarest. "I've worked on ships before."

Sheyan smiled. "That is probably a lie," he said mildly. "Those who ride Middle rarely do anything else. But could you perform a handler's duties?"

"It was no lie," said Dumarest. "And the answer is yes."

Abruptly Sheyan made his decision. "This is a rough ship. A small ship. Snatching the trade others manage without. Short journeys, mostly, planet hopping with freight and such, heavy loads and hard work. You'll be paid like the rest of us, with a share of the profit. Sometimes we make a pile, but mostly we break even. At times we carry passengers who like to gamble. If you accommodate them I get a half of the profit."

"And if I lose?"

"If you can't win then don't play." Sheyan leaned forward and rested his arms on his desk. "Work hard, be willing, and cause no trouble. That way we'll get along. Questions?"

"When do we leave?"

"Soon. You'll find a uniform in Elgart's cabin." The captain looked curiously at his new handler. "Aren't you interested as to where we are bound?"

"I'll find out," said Dumarest, "when we get there."

The steward guided him to the cabin. He was young, recent to space with a voice which had barely broken, but already his eyes held a flowering hardness.

"Elgart was a pig," he said as he led the way from the captain's office. "Mean and close and hard to get along with. I'm glad he's dead."

Dumarest made no comment. Instead he looked at the walls and ceiling of the passage down which they passed. The plastic carried a thin patina of grime and was marked with a mesh of scratches. The floor was heavily scuffed, uneven in places, and showing signs of wear and neglect.

"My name is Linardo del Froshure del Brachontari del Hershray Klarge," said the steward as they reached the cabin door. "But everyone calls me Lin. Will it be all right for me to call you Earl?"

"I've no objection." Dumarest pushed open the door of the cabin and passed inside. It was as he'd expected: a bare room fitted with a bunk, a chair, a small table. Cabinets filled one wall; the others bore lurid photographs of naked women. A scrap of carpet, frayed, covered the floor, and a player stood on the table. He switched it on and the thin, piping strains of cazendal music filled the air.

"Elgart was a funny one," commented Lin. "That music and this other stuff." His eyes moved to the photographs. "A real weird."

Dumarest switched off the player. "How many in the crew?"

"Five. You've met the captain. Nimino's the navigator and Claude's the engineer. Both are out on business, but you'll meet them later. Nimino's another weird and Claude likes the bottle." The steward's eyes dropped to Dumarest's left hand, to the ring on his third finger. "Say, that's quite a thing you've got there."

"The ring?" Dumarest glanced at it, the flat, red stone set in the heavy band. "It was a gift from a friend."

"Some friend!" Lin was envious. "I wish I had friends like that. You're wearing the cost of a double High passage at least." He leaned forward so as to study the ring more closely. "My uncle's a lapidary," he explained. "He taught me something about gems. That was before my old man got himself killed and I had to earn a living. I think he wanted me to join him in the business, but what the hell! Who wants to spend their lives stuck in a shop? My chance came and I grabbed it while it was going. Another few years and I'll become an officer. Then for the big ships and the wide-open life."

"Is that what you want?"

"Sure. What could be better?"

It was the defiance of youth, but Dumarest knew what the youngster didn't. The wide-open life he dreamed of was nothing but an endless journeying between the stars, constantly bounded by the monotony of imprisoning walls. The years slipping past broken only by planetfalls and brief dissipation. Those who rode Middle lived lives of incredible restriction despite the journeys they made. Too often they found refuge in strange diversions and perverted pleasures.

"So you haven't been very long on the *Moray?*"

"No," Lin admitted. "But it's the best kind of life a man could have. Moving, traveling, seeing new things all the time. Always gambling that the cargo you're carrying will be the one to hit the jackpot. At least," he amended, "it is in the Web."

"Is that where you're from?"

"Sure. Laconis. You've heard of it?"

"No," said Dumarest. He looked thoughtfully at the steward. The boy was eager to enhance his stature by imparting information. It would do no harm to encourage him and perhaps do some good. "Tell me about it."

Lin shrugged. "There isn't much to tell. It's just a place. Some agriculture, a little industry, some trading. Mostly we mine the ridges for rare metals and gems, but that's for prospectors, mostly. The yield is too low for a big operation. There's some fishing, but nothing special. It's just a place like most of the Web worlds. You'll see."

Dumarest frowned. "Is that where we're bound? The Web?"

"Didn't you know?"

"It's a long way from here. What's the *Moray* doing on Aarn if it's a Web trader?"

"The engines went on the blink." Lin was casual. "The old man managed to get a cargo and decided to have a refit. The stuff barely paid for the energy to haul it, but at least we got here for free. And you don't get Erhaft generators as cheap as you can get them on Aarn."

"New generators?"

"Hell, no!" Lin was disgusted. "We could have got those in the Web. Reconditioned—but they'll do the job. Claude checked them out and he's satisfied. After all, it's his neck too."

"Yes," said Dumarest dryly. "Let's hope that he remembered that."

"Meaning?"

The boy was star-struck, despite his superficial hardness. His head was filled with dreams and he was unable to recognize unpalatable truths. He would learn fast—if he did not die before the opportunity to learn presented itself. Dumarest was harsh as he looked at the steward.

"Meaning that he may not intend to rejoin the ship. That he could have been drunk at a critical time or, if not drunk, had his mind on a bottle instead of the job at hand. Damn it, boy, grow up! The universe isn't a place of heroes! Men are what they are and no one is perfect."

"Claude wouldn't do a thing like that." Lin's eyes betrayed his uncertainty. "He likes to drink, sure, but where's the harm in that? And he teaches me things. Anyway," he added triumphantly, "the old man wouldn't stick his neck out like that. There's nothing wrong with those generators. There can't be."

"Then where's the engineer?"

"I told you. He's out looking for business with Nimino."

"That's right," agreed Dumarest. "A weird out with a drunk. A happy combination. This trip should show us a lot of profit." He stressed the plural so as to let the boy know that he considered himself a part of the crew and, as such, had a right to be critical. "Do you think they'll find any?"

"I don't know," admitted the steward. "I doubt if Nimino will bother much. He's probably spending his time at some revival or other. He's religious," he explained. "I don't mean that he's a member of the Universal Church. He's that and a lot more. He dabbles in every cult going. Transmigration, Reincarnation, Starcom, Extravitalis, Satanism, Planarism, Amorphism—you name it and he's interested. His cabin's full of charms and fetishs, idols and symbols, sympathetic relationship mandalas and inspired pictographs. When I said he was a weird that's what I meant."

"And Claude?"

"If there's a load to be found in a tavern then he'll find it," said the steward. "He got us a few crates of machine patterns—you'll have to check the temperature of those—strain-impressed molecular structure designs in a protoplasmic gel. And he managed to pick up some new sonic drill recordings."

"Speculative buying," said Dumarest. "Just the sort of thing a drunk would find himself landed with. Anything concrete in the nature of paying freight?"

"Not as yet," said Lin reluctantly. "But don't get the wrong impression about Claude. He may appear to buy wild, but the things he gets have value in the Web. Ships aren't frequent out there, don't forget, and we call at a lot of minor worlds. I've known us to make a 1,000 percent profit on stuff you wouldn't look at twice on a planet like Aarn."

"All right," said Dumarest. "I'll take your word for it."

"They're good," insisted the boy. "Odd, maybe, but good. You just don't know."

Dumarest smiled. "I'm a little edgy and maybe too critical. You know them better than I do. How long before we leave?"

The steward glanced at his wrist. "A couple of hours. Nimino will be back a good hour before then. Like to make a little bet?"

"Such as?"

"Even money that Claude doesn't come back empty-handed. Five stergols. Is it a bet?"

"It's a bet." Dumarest looked around the cabin. "Now, maybe, you'd better leave me to check my gear."

Alone, he tore the photographs from the walls, frowning at the lighter patches they left behind. A cabinet held a uniform and a suit of rough, protective clothing such as was worn by field loaders. Both were in stretch material, neither were as clean as they could have been. The uniform cap was battered, the visor cracked, and the sweatband stained and thick with grease. The late handler had not been a finicky man.

Other cabinets showed a pile of books in plain covers.

Dumarest flipped one open and listened to the soft obscenities whispering from the illustrated pages. Both voice and moving illustrations died as he closed the book and reached for another. They were all of the same type. A stack of recordings held cazenda music. A three-dimensional jigsaw lay in scattered pieces beside a chessboard and men. The pieces were of lambent crystal, intricately carved and of obvious worth. The board was an electronic instrument for the replaying of recorded games. A box held a few items of personal significance: a ring, a locket containing a curl of hair, a certificate issued by the medical council of Octarge, a pair of dice fashioned from animal bone, scraps and fragments of a man's entire life.

Dumarest looked further. A small compartment held a hypogun—the butt worn and the instrument almost certainly poorly calibrated. Boxes held ampules of drugs which could be blasted by air pressure through clothing, skin, and fat directly into the bloodstream; quicktime, slowtime, antibiotics, compounds for the relief of pain, the bringing of sleep, and the ease of tension. A shabby case held gleaming surgical instruments, and a thick book was an illustrated medical manual. Obviously, on this vessel, the handler was expected to double as physician.

Taking a handful of disposable tissues, Dumarest soaked them with sterilizing solution and swabbed the neck, wrists, and crotch of the uniform and protective clothing. Taking fresh tissues he wiped the sweatband of the uniform cap until it was free of dirt and grease.

Satisfied, he stripped off his tunic. The light from the overhead glowtube shone on the hard whiteness of his skin, throwing thin lines of scar tissue into prominence over chest and arms. The hilt of a knife showed above the waistband of his pants, the nine-inch blade gleaming as he threw it beside the tunic on the bed. The pants followed, and he stood naked aside from snug shorts.

Dressed in the uniform, he took up his own things, folded them, and stuffed them into a cabinet. Carefully he adjusted the uniform cap until the cracked visor shielded his eyes and then, after a final inspection, left the cabin and made for the section of the ship which was his responsibility.

Like the cabin, it was as he'd expected. The banks of sterilizing ultraviolet lamps showed dark patches where units needed replacing. The caskets in which livestock were transported showed obvious signs of lengthy disuse, and several of the cargo restraints were inoperative. He paused beside the crates of machine patterns, checking the temperature against the thermostat setting. There was a three-degree difference on the wrong side and he changed the setting hoping that the cargo had not suffered damage.

Thoughtfully he made his way to the salon. Here the passengers, if any, would spend their recreational time—which meant all of it on short journeys—drawing their ration of basic from a spigot on the wall. That, at least, was functioning as it should and he drew a cup of the thick mixture, sipping the warm compound of glucose, protein, and vitamins as he studied the furnishings.

"Pretty rough, aren't they?" Dumarest turned and looked at the man who had silently entered the salon. He was middle-aged, his face thin beneath his uniform cap, his eyes startlingly direct. The insignia on collar and breast was that of a navigator. "My name's Nimino." He held out his hand. "You're Earl Dumarest. The captain told me we had a new handler. Welcome aboard."

His handclasp was firm, the skin dry and febrile. "Well, what do you think of the *Moray?*"

She was a bad ship in bad condition. Five men were too few to crew such a vessel, small though she was. Maintenance suffered and the outward dirt was a sure sign of inner neglect. Dumarest took another sip of basic and said, "I've seen ships in worse condition."

"In a scrapyard," agreed Nimino. "So have I. But as operating vessels in space?" He shrugged. "There could be worse tucked away in some forgotten corner of the galaxy, but I doubt it. Certainly there are none in the Web. Each time we commence a journey we take a gamble with death and our profit, if any, is earned with tears of blood."

"Then why stay with her?"

"Why not? If death is waiting to claim a man—what difference where he may be? And then again, my friend, perhaps, like you, I have little choice." The navigator glanced at the cup in Dumarest's hand. "Hungry so soon?"

"No."

"The habit of a traveler then," said Nimino, smiling. "Eat while there is food available for you never can be certain as to when you may have the opportunity to eat again. If nothing else, Earl, it tells me what you are."

Dumarest finished the contents of the cup and dropped it into the receptacle provided. "And you?"

"I am a weird, didn't Lin tell you that? I believe that there is more to the scheme of things than a man can perceive with his limited senses. Electro-magnetic radiation for example. Can a man see infrared or ultraviolet? Tell the presence of radio waves, of magnetism, of the ebb and flow of the energies of space without mechanical aid? Of course not. And yet still men deny that there could be higher realms of existence than those we know. You are interested in such things?"

"No."

"Then you also think that I am a weird?"

"I don't give a damn what you are," said Dumarest bluntly. "Just as long as you're a good navigator."

Nimino laughed. "At least you are honest, my friend. Have no fear, I know my trade. And I know the Web, which is a thing few men can say without boasting. As long as the generators do not fail, I can take the *Moray* where we want her to go. Unless fate decides otherwise," he added. "Against fate what chance has limited man?"

"In my experience those who talk of fate usually do so to provide themselves an excuse for failure," said Dumarest. The banality of the conversation was beginning to annoy him. The navigator's place was on the bridge, for until he gave the word the ship could not leave. "And it is wrong to rely on superior powers. Even if they existed, it would be wrong. Wrong and foolish. I do not think you are a foolish man."

"And I do not think you are wholly what you seem." Nimino smiled again, his teeth flashing in the cavern of his mouth, startlingly white against the rich darkness of his skin. "Certainly you are not a common traveler, and few handlers trouble themselves with philosophical concepts. But enough of this wrangling. We are shipmates for good or ill and we both have our duties. Until later, my friend. I anticipate many pleasant hours."

Fifty-seven minutes later they left Aarn, rising on the magic of the Erhaft field from the ground, through the atmosphere, and up into space where their sensors quested for target stars.

Twenty-six minutes after that, Dumarest paid five stergols to the steward.

Lin had won his bet. Claude had found them a passenger.

II

HE WAS A round, sleek, yellow-skinned man of indeterminate age, who smiled often and spoke at length. Gems glittered on his pudged hands and soft fabric of price clothed his rotund body. His hair was a cropped stubble on the ball of his skull and his eyes, slanted like almonds, were as watchful as a cat's. His name was Yalung and he claimed to be a dealer in precious stones.

Dumarest thought about him as he worked on the caskets. Carefully he checked each connection and tested each seal, measuring the degree of chill established by the refrigeration, counting the seconds as the eddy currents warmed the interior of the coffinlike boxes. Several times he made adjustments, knowing that a human life could depend on his skill. Animals had a wider tolerance than men, but animals did not always fill the caskets.

Claude entered the region as Dumarest straightened from the last of the caskets.

"All finished?"

"Yes." Dumarest handed the engineer the meters he had borrowed. "I'll check the rest of the equipment later. Can you make some more restraints for the cargo?"

"Why bother? We don't carry much and what we do won't come to any hurt."

"Can you make them?"

"Later." The engineer leaned against the curved metal of the wall and blinked his bloodshot eyes. He had been drinking and his broad, mottled face was heavy with the red mesh of burst capillaries. "You worry too much, Earl. Elgart never used to worry like you do."

"Maybe that's why he's dead," said Dumarest dryly.

"He died because he was a perverted swine," said Claude dispassionately. "I've no objection to a man being a lecher, but he was worse than that. Once when we carried some animals he—well, never mind. He's dead and good riddance. Like a drink?"

It was wine: thin, sharp with too much acid, the flavor indistinguishable. Dumarest sipped and watched as the engineer gulped. Behind him, squatting on thick bed-plates, the generators emitted a quivering ultrasonic song of power, the inaudible sound transmuted by the metal of the hull into a barely noticed vibration.

"Swill," said Claude as he lowered his empty glass. "Some cheap muck I bought on Aarn. They don't know how to make wine. Now on Vine they make a wine which would wake the dead. Thick and rich and with the color of blood. A man could live on the wine of Vine. Live and die on it and never regret wasted opportunities."

Dumarest said softly, "As you do?"

"I was there once," said the engineer as if he had not heard the interjection. "At harvest time. The girls carried in the grapes and trod them beneath their bare feet. The juice stained their legs and thighs, red on white and olive, thick juice on soft and tender flesh. As the day grew warmer they threw off all their clothes and rolled naked among the fruit. It was a time of love and passion, kissing and copulating in great vats of succulent grapes, the juice spurting and staining everyone so that all looked like creatures of nature."

Dumarest took a little more wine, waiting for the engineer to extinguish his dream.

"There was a girl," whispered Claude. "Soft and young and as white as the snows found on the hills of Candaris. We trod the grapes together and joined bodies as we mated in the juice. For a week we loved beneath the sun and the stars with wine flowing like water and others all around laughing and singing and laving their bodies with the juice. The harvest on the following season must have been exceptional if what they believed was true."

"Fertility rites," said Dumarest. "I understand."

"You understand." The engineer poured himself more of the thin wine. "I did not. I thought she loved me for myself alone, not because she thought that a stranger would bring fresh seed to the mating, new energy to the fields. For a week she was mine and then it was over." He gulped the wine and stared broodingly into the glass. "Often I wonder if my grandsons tread the grapes as I did, if my granddaughters yield themselves as did she."

"You could find out," suggested Dumarest. "You could go back."

"No. That is a thing no man should ever do. The past is dead, forget it, let us instead drink to the future."

18

"To the future," said Dumarest, and sipped a little more wine. "Tell me about our passenger."

"Yalung?" Claude blinked as he strove to focus his attention. "He is just a man."

"How did you meet?"

"In a tavern. I was looking for business and he approached me. He had money and wanted a High passage to the Web."

"It's just as well he didn't want to travel Low," said Dumarest. "He would never have made it."

"The caskets?" Claude shrugged. "We rarely use them; the journey between planets is too short. Even on the longer trips Sheyan usually adjusts the price and lets any passengers ride under quicktime. The Web is compact," he explained. "Stars are relatively close. Anyway, we don't often carry passengers."

"Let's talk about the one we have now."

"What is there to talk about? He wanted a passage and could pay for it. He approached me. What else is there to know?"

"He approached you." Dumarest was thoughtful. "Didn't you think it strange? A man with money for a High passage wanting to travel on a ship like this?"

Claude frowned, thinking. "No," he said after a while. "It isn't strange. Not many ships head for the Web and those that do only go to established planets, the big worlds with money, trade, and commerce. From there shuttle vessels take freight and passengers to the other planets. Yalung wants to roam the Web and this is the best way for him to do it."

"So he intends to stay with us?"

"That's what he said." Claude chuckled as he looked at Dumarest. "He hasn't really any choice. I told you that ships are few in the Web. You could be stranded on a planet for months waiting for a vessel, and then you'd have to go where it took you. That's where we come in. Charter, special freight, speculative trading, things like that. We could maybe touch a score of worlds before landing at one of the big termini." His smile grew wider as he saw the other's expression. "Didn't Sheyan tell you?"

"The details? No."

"He wouldn't. He needed a handler more than he needed to teach the innocent. But it isn't so bad. We'll get along

and could even have a little fun. You'll get used to it, Earl.
You might even get to like the life."

"Like you?"

Claude lost his smile as he groped for the bottle. "No,
Earl, not like me. But then you don't have to be like me. No
one does."

No one, thought Dumarest as he left the engineer to his
anodyne. Not Nimino who found his refuge in religion, or
Sheyan who had his command if nothing else. Not Lin who
carried a headful of stars and who looked on danger as
a spice to living instead of the constant threat to existence
it really was. No one needed to hit the bottle—but sometimes it could help.

Dumarest washed and changed from the protective clothing he had worn while working on the caskets, changing
into his uniform and the cap with the cracked visor. His
soft shoes were soundless on the worn flooring as he made
his way towards the bridge. At the salon he halted and
looked inside. Yalung, the sole occupant, sat before a table
on which were spread a handful of variously colored crystals.
He held a pair of tweezers in one pudgy hand and his eyes
were narrowed as if to increase his vision.

He didn't move. Not even when Dumarest entered the
compartment and stood at his side. Still he sat like a man
of stone, not even his eyelids flickering, unconscious of the
man at his side. He looked dead but he was far from that.
He was living at a reduced tempo, the magic of quicktime
slowing his metabolism and time-awareness to a fraction of
normal. They had left Aarn two days ago, but to the passenger it was less than an hour.

Gently Dumarest reached out and touched the pudgy
hand, gently, for the relative speed of his hand could deal
a savage blow. The skin was firm, more youthful than it
seemed, the small indent vanishing as soon as he removed
the pressure.

Stooping he examined the scattered gems, noting the
trapped fire smoldering within their crystalline depths, the
perfection of facets and polish. They, at least, were genuine
—as was probably everything else about the passenger.
Yalung could be exactly what he claimed and his presence
on the ship due to nothing more than sheer coincidence.

Dumarest straightened and left the salon, making his way
to the bridge. He knocked and entered when Sheyan growled
a summons. The captain was alone, sitting in the big con-

trol chair, surrounded by instruments which did what no ordinary man could ever do. He looked very small in the confines of the chair, the box on his lap somehow seeming to accentuate his diminution. It was of metal, strongly chased and fitted with a combination lock. It could, probably, be smashed open but never rifled without leaving trace. He clung to it as if finding warmth and comfort from the decorated metal.

"You want something?"

"The caskets are now fully operational," said Dumarest. "Some minor work remains to be done on the cargo restraints, but that is all. Aside from a complete cleaning," he added. "I can't say anything about the rest of the ship."

"That's right." Sheyan twisted his head so as to stare at his handler. "Your job is to look after the cargo, not to tell me what needs to be done. And a little grime never killed anyone yet."

"That depends," said Dumarest, "on just where the grime is. I wouldn't care for it in an open wound, for example."

"The *Moray* is not an open wound."

"It isn't a very efficient ship either," said Dumarest bluntly. He looked about the control room. "Shouldn't the navigator be on duty?"

Sheyan reared up in his chair. "I decide who shall be on duty!" he snapped. "I am the captain. If you choose to forget it just remember what will happen if I decide you are insubordinate." He sank down again, his anger dissolving as rapidly as it had come. "You don't understand," he said. "You're thinking of the big ships with their big crews and the spit and polish they use to run them. The *Moray* isn't like that. A little dirt doesn't matter as long as the generators aren't affected. More crew means smaller shares and they are small enough as it is. Just ride along with us as we are and you'll be all right. Try fighting and it will get you nowhere."

Dumarest frowned, thinking of the man he had first met in the captain's office, comparing him with the man who now sat in the control chair. Physically they were the same, but somehow there was a difference. He had deliberately tried to ignite anger and had received, instead, a near apology. It was as if Sheyan had been cowed by something, his spirit crushed so that he wanted nothing more than to be left alone. Looking at the vision screens Dumarest could guess what it was.

Space was immense—the distances between the stars impossible to conceive by a human brain. The figures could be learned but they meant nothing; they were so vast as to be totally outside the limits of human comprehension. Light took years to travel between the stars; ships could do it faster but the distances remained the same. If anything could reduce a man's arrogance it was the cold indifference of the galaxy, the knowledge that in the universe he was less than a minute bacteria crawling on the face of creation.

Quietly he said, "Permission to use quicktime, captain?"

"What?" Sheyan jerked, his hands convulsive as they gripped the box. "Quicktime? Yes. Yes, by all means."

"A general issue?"

"Nimino has his own. I trust him to use it with discretion. You may give it to the rest."

"As you order, captain," said Dumarest. "And yourself?"

"No. I don't need it. That is, I don't want it." Again Sheyan's hands closed on the edges of his box. "That will be all, handler."

Alone, the captain relaxed in his chair, trying not to grip the box, to think of what it contained. Dumarest had annoyed him, upset him rather, but how could the man even begin to guess? Like the rest he was closed in by walls of metal, protected, shielded from what lay without. Only Nimino could really begin to understand because, like himself, the navigator stared with electronic eyes at the naked menace of the stars.

And they were menacing. They waited, confident in the knowledge that they must win, that they were greater than man and anything he could do. Let his ships probe among them, land on their worlds, diminish space by the magic of the Erhaft field, they would still conquer. They would always conquer because men were mortal and they were not. They could afford to wait and watch and, perhaps, glow a little brighter whenever a ship died.

As the *Moray* would die—and he with it.

He closed his eyes, trying to find in darkness the courage he seemed to lose each time they left a world. It was the inaction which caused it, he told himself. The necessity to do nothing but sit and wait for the one day that must surely come. A minor flaw in one of the instruments. A break in a component. A trifling error which would be magnified with distance until it became overwhelming. A little thing, any little thing, and he would be totally erased, killed, wiped out—his personal universe destroyed.

Extinction.

He gasped, shuddering, jerking open his eyes to look again at the shimmering splendor of the stars which hung in scattered profusion. Shining points, sheets, curtains and haloes of magnificent luminescence dulled, directly ahead, by the somber black cloud which held the Web. He stared at it, hating the darkness, knowing it to be a waiting trap for the unwary. Perhaps this time?

"No!" Sheyan reared up in his chair, sweat beading his face as he fought his own imagination. "No!"

The sound of his own voice was a comfort and he looked around, forcing himself to check the silent machines which filled the control room, the computers and sensors, the mechanical pilots with their programmed navigational tapes, the telltales which gave him information about the ship itself.

Tiny lights winked back at him, red and green, blue and yellow, dull orange and flaring white. A ripple of color and movement as vectors were checked, slight adjustments made, the currents of space ridden as a ship would ride a turbulent sea. And space was a sea, a three-dimensional ocean of electronic wind and magnetic storm, the dead residue of solar flares and vanished novae sweeping endlessly through the gulf like wreckage and flotsam, antimatter and vicious gusts of killing radiation.

All met and neutralized by the silent efficiency of the machines among which he sat.

Ships don't need captains, he thought. Navigators, perhaps, and even engineers—but not captains. What could I do if something went wrong? What could anyone do? But ships were not always in space and someone had to be in command, to make the decisions and to give the orders and see they were carried out. A ship was more than just a hull and engines and a mass of complex equipment. A ship was all that and more. Men still had to serve and a man still had to be in charge.

But men were weak. Sometimes too weak and then, when alone, they began to break. Slowly, at first, but always in one direction. And once they cracked, they could never be repaired.

Sheyan straightened, grabbing the box as it threatened to fall from his lap, snatching a handkerchief from his pocket and wiping the sweat from his face. Two days, he thought. Only two days and already you're going under. Make it three at least, four even, five if you can. Use quicktime like the others do and shorten the journey to a fraction of its real time. No man should be expected to stare needlessly at the stars.

Not unless he had aid.

His fingers trembled as he turned the dial of the combination. It was a simple setting, three numbers only, and within seconds the lid rose with a soft click. Inside the box something moved, sluggishly, then quickened to pulsing life as it felt the warmth of his hand.

The box, empty, fell to one side as Sheyan relaxed, breathing easily, lost in a cloud of euphoric dreams.

"The Web," said Yalung, smiling. "A fascinating place. You must know it well."

"No," said Dumarest. "I have never been there."

"Then you are new on this ship?"

"Yes." Dumarest was telling the man nothing he probably didn't already know or could easily find out. And he would find out. Yalung was a curious man. "Have you?"

"Once, many years ago; but it was a brief visit only and there was much that I did not see."

"In the Web," said Nimino, "there is much that no man has seen. Not even those who have lived their lives on one of its worlds. Am I not right, Lin?"

The steward nodded, pleased at having been brought into the conversation. The four were seated at the table in the salon, keeping the trader company as was the custom when passengers were few. All held cups of basic and a deck of cards lay between them. Idly, Dumarest stirred them with the tip of a finger.

"Tell me about it," he said. "There seems to be much that I should know."

"About the Web?" Lin shrugged, acting older than his years. "It's just a place like any other. Stars and planets and people who live on them. It seemed normal enough to me."

"You come from Laconis, which is near the edge," said Nimino. "And you joined us on our way out. Wait until we get deep into the system before you talk about it being normal. The Web is a cloud of primeval dust," he explained to Dumarest. "Within it, the stars are very close and each star has many worlds. For trading it is ideal for the journeys are short and the needs of the people great. At least it would be ideal if conditions were as they are in normal space. But the area within the cloud is not normal. The stars are too close. There are vicious gravitational crosscurrents, magnetic storms of incredible violence, ionic displays, and other unpleasant phenonema. You have dealt with our caskets and you know what eddy currents can do. Imagine them on an interstellar scale. Imagine also, the sleeting radiation, the very warping of space which occurs in areas close to double stars and you will have some idea as to conditions facing ships which probe too deeply into the Web."

"They are bad," said Yalung softly. "Very bad. On my last trip I heard news of two vessels which had failed to complete their journeys. One, it was said, fell into a star. The other had been found, a mass of twisted wreckage, the fabric having been apparently turned inside out. No one chose to guess what had really happened."

"And yet you return," said Dumarest quietly. "Why do that if the area is so dangerous?"

"For the same reason this ship returns." Yalung's smile was bland. "For profit. I am a dealer in precious stones and my trade is not without competition. In the Web are many worlds and on them could be gems of price. With conditions being what they are, it should be simple for a man to buy low and later sell high."

"There are gems on Laconis," said Lin quickly. "I could introduce you to my uncle. He would give you a fair bargain."

Again Yalung gave his bland smile. "I shall remember your offer if ever we land on the planet," he said. "But, meaning no disrespect, your knowledge of gems can hardly be large."

"It's larger than you think. Earl, show him your ring." Lin frowned as Dumarest made no move to obey. "Please, Earl. Show him your ring."

Slowly Dumarest lifted his left hand and rested it on the pack of cards. The overhead light caught the stone and turned it into the likeness of an oval of freshly spilled blood. His eyes were watchful as the boy touched the ring, fastened on the trader's face, alert to catch the slightest change of expression. Lin's foolish boasting might have an unexpected bonus.

"A fine stone," said Yalung casually. "Fine but hardly

rare. Together with the mount it would be worth, perhaps, the cost of a short High passage."

"Think again," said Lin. "I know stones. This is worth double what you say."

"Perhaps." Yellow silk moved as the trader lifted his shoulders, the black glyphs with which it was decorated moving like slumbering serpents. "But you forget, my young friend, I am a trader and never enhance the price."

"But I am right?"

"You are right. The ring is worth what you say, and I must congratulate you on your knowledge. And now, perhaps, someone would care to indulge my pleasure in a game of cards?" Yalung looked from one to the other. "No? You are tired, perhaps? I hardly think that the crew of a ship like this would have moral objections to gambling."

"No," said Lin quickly. "I—"

"Will go to bed." Dumarest was curt in his interruption. "Take a cup of basic to the engineer, another to the captain, and then retire."

"But, Earl—"

"Do as I say." Dumarest watched as the boy drew a single cup of liquid from the spigot. "What about the captain?"

"He doesn't need any. Am I right, Nimino?"

"That is correct." The navigator looked at Dumarest. "Sheyan takes care of himself during a flight and brooks no interruption. Take the cup to the engineer, Lin, and then retire." He watched as the steward left the salon. "You were hard on the boy," he said quietly. "He is young."

Dumarest agreed. "Too young to ape the man and far too young to gamble with those who would take all he owns."

"And too young, perhaps, to call attention to a ring?" Yalung's voice was a purr. "It was bad manners, I grant, and bad manners must be punished. But to shame the lad? It would not have hurt him to play a little. The stakes need not have been high."

"If the stakes are low then it is not a gamble," said Nimino. "A man cannot lose what he doesn't care to keep. And you are mistaken as to Earl's motives. Why should he object to Lin showing you his ring?"

"Did I give that impression?" Yalung spread his hands, his smile deprecating. "My apologies if I did; it was unconscious, I assure you. But on Aarn there was talk about a man wearing a ring and another man found dead in a closet in his room. The dead man was a known thief and the assumption is that he died in pursuit of his trade. It is a rumor, you understand, a whisper in the taverns. You may have heard it?"

"No," said Dumarest tightly. "I did not."

"Then again I am mistaken. I thought that you were a little tender on the subject—no man likes to be associated with murder. But, of course, the association can be nothing but coincidence. Many men wear rings."

"I wear one myself," said Nimino thrusting forward his hand. The light shone from a golden snake coiled around his finger. "Would you care to value it, trader?"

"In terms of its true worth or its sentimental attachment?"

"Neither. In terms of its protective power." The navigator smiled as he lowered his hand. "You hesitate. Well, that is to be expected from one who deals in money, what could you know of the value of spiritual things? Yet you haven't the price of this ring should you want to buy it from me. It was given me by the Decal Ghengian himself and all he touched was holy."

Yalung's eyes held a gleam of amusement as he glanced at Dumarest. "Then the ring must be very valuable," he said gently. "For the Decal Ghengian will touch things no more."

"He has found the Way?" Nimino was excited. "He has found the realm beyond?"

"As well as any man can find it. He is dead. Killed by a fall from the roof of his hotel in Nagash on Jacellon. Some say that he was drunk and attempted to fly. Others that he was summoned. A few whisper that he was assassinated, but that is rumor and rumor always lies."

"Dead." Nimino looked down at his ring and touched it with loving fingers. "Had he lived what might not that man have accomplished. He could even have found the holy world from which all men originated."

"Now that, at least, you cannot believe," said Yalung. "It is the stuff of legend and as frail as gossamer. Forgive me if I lose patience but I have heard such legends too often to be tolerant. The mystery planets found and lost again: Jackpot, Bonanza, El Dorado, a dozen others. Worlds of dreams and imagination born of longing and dying hope. I have traveled the galaxy and have never heard more than a rumor of any of them."

Dumarest looked down at his hands, then at those of the trader. Quietly he said, "Have you ever heard of Earth?"

"Earth?" Yalung's hands remained immobile. His eyes were enigmatic as Dumarest raised his head to stare into the yellow face. "A strange name for a world. I know of Sand, an odd place of almost total desert. A species of insect lives beneath the surface and constructs balls of natural secretions which have a slight value when ground and polished. But Earth? No."

"And you, Nimino?"

The navigator hesitated. "There are so many worlds—how can one man know them all? The name is strange to me, Earl, yet I cannot say there is no such place."

"How about Terra? Is that name familiar?" Dumarest shrugged as both men shook their heads. "Well, never mind. It isn't important."

Not if a life had no value and years of searching were of no account. Not if home meant nothing to a man or a quest had no substance. The questions had been automatic, born of the hope that someone, somewhere, would be able to give a positive answer. It was a slim chance, but one which had to be tried. Their response was another disappointment to add to the rest.

Dumarest picked up the deck of cards. "Well, gentlemen," he said. "Shall we play?"

III

DUMAREST STOOD at the head of the loading ramp and looked over the landing field at Hendris. It was small and, aside from the *Moray*, deserted. An acre of gritty soil lacking the usual perimeter fence, the surface scarred and blotched with weed. To one side a huddle of shacks stood in the shadow of a gaunt warehouse, flimsy structures advertising their poverty. More substantial buildings rested further back in the town, a listless flag signaling the whereabouts of a tavern. Edging the field a squat tower held the administration offices, the flat roof surmounted by the elaborate antennae of a supraradio.

A flash of yellow moved from the building: Yalung, probably on his way to search for precious gems. Thoughtfully

Dumarest looked at the sky. It was dark, almost indigo, the ball of the sun halfway towards the horizon. It was a dull, angry red, the wide corona limned with sooty markings, the surface writhing as it fed on the dust. From a few parsecs it would be invisible, all radiation absorbed by the cloud before it could escape from the Web.

"Hey there!"

Dumarest looked down. A field loader had come from behind the vessel riding an antigrav raft loaded high with crates. He stared upwards, squinting.

"You the handler?"

"That's right."

"What happened to Elgart? I thought he was Sheyan's man."

"He was."

"Like that, eh?" The field loader shrugged. "Well, it's none of my business. You ready to take delivery?"

"Just a minute." Dumarest walked down the ramp until he stood level with the man. "When did the last ship leave here?"

"Three days ago. Heading Inside."

"And before that?"

"Maybe two weeks. Heading Inside." The man grinned. "I know what you're after, a ship out. Well, mister, you're not the only one. Sam Glegan at the hotel is getting fat on traders waiting to be carried out of the Web. It's been two months since the last ship headed that way and it could be as long again until the next."

Dumarest frowned. "Where's the next terminal?"

"Thermyle? That's in the next system. You could pick up a ship bound for there in maybe a month or so. Maybe less. They don't run much to schedule. Why the interest? You thinking of quitting the *Moray*?"

"Forget it." Dumarest looked at the crates. "Are they for us?"

"That's right. And there's three times as much waiting to be hauled. Where do you want it?"

"In the hold."

"Open up the hull and I'll oblige," said the field loader. "Failing that I can't do more than dump it. My job is to deliver it to the ship. How you get it inside is your problem." He guided the raft to the foot of the ramp and released the grapnels. Bobbing, the vehicle rose, an open frame behind the driver's seat. "Right," he said. "It's all yours."

The crates contained agricultural implements: hoes, ax heads, saw blades, scythes, plowshares, and rakes, together with rods and ingots of native iron. Each crate was heavier than the weight of a man. Dumarest lifted one and let it fall with a crash on the foot of the ramp. On normal vessels the loading ramp would have been powered, hooks and rollers carrying the cargo up to the hold where it could be stacked. On the *Moray* the power attachment refused to work.

The field loader delivered the second heap of crates as Dumarest walked from the vessel. He paused at the edge of the field looking to either side. Usually there would have been men looking for either work or passage but Hendris was a casual world and to wait for a ship was to starve. The edge of the field was deserted and Dumarest walked on to where the drooping flag hung over the tavern.

"Earl!" Claude shouted an invitation as he entered the long, bleak room. "Come and join me!"

The engineer sat slumped at one end of the bar, his broad, mottled face streaming with perspiration. One big hand was clamped around a tankard of fused sand. At his side Lin hovered, an attendant shadow. A straggle of men filled the rest of the place, most of them standing close to where Claude was sitting.

"Earl!" he shouted again. "Come and join me and my friends." His free hand thudded on the bar. "A drink for the handler!"

Dumarest ignored the foaming tankard the bartender slapped down before him. He said, "Claude, I want you back at the ship. The loading ramp isn't working."

"Why tell me?" The engineer emptied his tankard and reached for the one served to Dumarest. "The cargo's your job."

"And the ramp is yours. I'm not going to sweat because a fat, drunken slob is too lazy to do his work. Now get on your feet and get to it!"

Claude slowly rose from his stool, one big hand clenching the tankard. Thickly he said, "What did you call me?"

"A fat, drunken slob," said Lin. "I heard him."

"You stay out of this!" Dumarest didn't look at the steward. Around him he heard the scuff of boots as men retreated.

"A fat, drunken slob," said Claude softly. "A fat—"

His bulk belied his speed. He turned, his arm a blur as

he smashed the edge of the tankard down on the counter, rising with a circle of jagged shards, thrusting them viciously at Dumarest's face. Dumarest lifted his left hand, his palm smacking against the wrist, gripping, holding it firm—the broken tankard inches from his eyes. He could see the savage points, the little flecks of brightness in the fused sand, and thought of what the improvised weapon could do, what one similar to it had done on Aarn.

He twisted and, as the shattered tankard dropped to the floor, balled his right fist and struck at Claude's jaw.

"All right," he said to Lin as the engineer fell. "When he wakes up get him back to the ship." To the others standing around he said, "You've helped him to drink his pay, now you can help him to do his work. I want six men to load the *Moray*. You six. Let's get on with it."

Nimino entered the hold as Dumarest was securing the last of the cargo. He stood by the open port, his slim figure silhouetted against the angry ball of the sun, the darkness of his skin merging with the darkness of shadow. Teeth and eyes caught reflected light and made touches of transient brilliance, fading gleams accentuated by the movements of his hand, the polish of his nails.

"I hear that you've been having a little trouble, Earl."

Dumarest lifted a crate and swung it into position. "Nothing that I would call trouble."

"No? Lin tells it differently. He is entranced by the manner in which you co-opted labor to move the cargo. And he is bemused by the speed of your movements. The way in which you caught Claude's wrist. To hear him relate the story is to believe that you moved far more quickly than is considered possible."

"Lin is young," said Dumarest.

"And the young tend to exaggerate." Nimino moved a little, resting his shoulder on the edge of the open port. "True, but the facts remain. Have you ever undergone specialized training? I ask because the school of Jengha Dal teaches a system by which the reflexes can be accelerated. Do you know of it?"

"No."

"Perhaps your formative years were spent on a world of excessive gravity," mused the navigator. "But no, your physical development contradicts that supposition. As your strength contradicts the assumption that you are a common traveler who chooses to work a passage from fear of riding Low."

Dumarest stacked the final crate and turned to look at the navigator. "Did I say that?"

"Sheyan assumed it; but, of course, he was wrong. Those who travel Low have little body fat and less strength. The caskets enfeeble them. You are far from feeble."

"And you are too curious," said Dumarest flatly.

"Perhaps, my friend, but it is said that the path to knowledge lies through the asking of many questions. For example, I ask myself why a man such as you should have been in such a hurry to leave Aarn. For fear of a man? A woman? I think not and yet you chose to leave on a ship like this. Perhaps Fate was pressing at your heels, in which case a man has no choice. But, again, why on a ship like this? Your experience must have told you what the *Moray* is. A scavenger sweeping between close-set stars. Lin joined us, true, but he knew no better. Claude had no choice and Sheyan is snared in an economic trap."

"And you?"

Nimino shrugged. "An astrologer predicted that I should find great knowledge in a cloud of dust. The Web is such a cloud."

"And the knowledge?"

"Is still to come."

Some knowledge, perhaps, but the navigator would be learned in the ways of trading. And perhaps more. He could easily be a sensitive, a clairvoyant able to peer into the future, or a telepath with the skill of reading minds; or perhaps he could sense impending danger as an animal would sense the approach of a hunter. Or he could simply be highly curious and inordinately suspicious.

"It will come," said Dumarest. "When the time is ripe. Until then it could be a good idea to concentrate on your books."

"You dislike my curiosity?"

"I dislike anything which seems to have no purpose," said Dumarest. "And I cannot understand why you should be interested in me."

"In the Web a man needs to know with whom he travels," said Nimino quietly. "A little you have shown of yourself. Not much, but a little. For example I now know that you are not easily cowed. That you are accustomed to violence. That your reflexes are amazingly fast and that you are look-

ing for something. A planet named Earth. Well, wherever
it is you will not find it in the Web. I would venture to
guess that, by mischance or the workings of fate, you have
found yourself in a blind alley. The *Moray* is not an easy
ship to leave."

Not easy but neither was it hard; Dumarest could walk
off now, but what then? Weeks and perhaps months of
waiting stuck on this barely colonized world, exposed to
anyone who wanted to find him, vulnerable if they should.
He shrugged, trying to throw off the feeling which had followed him from world to world and was with him still. The
sense that someone was at his back, watching, waiting to
pounce. And it was not wholly a thing of imagination. The
dead man Yalung had spoken about. He had been a thief
and Dumarest had stunned and tied him fast. Later he had
found him dead and had gone immediately to the field.
Luck had seemed to favor him when the handler had been
murdered in the tavern but now he wasn't so sure.

Luck—or design?

And, if the latter, why?

"You are thinking, Earl," said Nimino breaking the silence. "What about? The cargo?"

Dumarest was willing to change the subject. "It's heavy."

"And valuable, despite what you are probably thinking.
We traded the machine patterns for it and the buyer must
have been satisfied to have delivered the goods so promptly."
The navigator stepped deeper into the hold and kicked one
of the crates. "Iron," he said. "Many of the inner worlds
lack heavy metals and some of them need the oxide in order
to provide trace-elements in the soil. We shall turn this load
with profit. They are poor worlds, Earl. Starvation planets
for the most part, colonized by mischance rather than intent.
Surely you have come across such worlds before?"

Backward planets at the end of the line. Dead worlds
without industry or work for transients, making it impossible
for them to gather the cost of a Low passage.

"I've seen a few," said Dumarest. "They are bad places
for a traveler to find."

"No world is a good one on which to be stranded,"
agreed Nimino. "You must tell me about them some day. In
return I will tell you of Clothon, of Landkis and Brame.
Sacred places all. Planets which have known the tread of
those closer to the Ultimate than we. Holy places."

"Each world is a holy place," said Dumarest quietly. "To those who believe it so."

"And Earth? Is that mysterious world such a place?"

"Perhaps." Dumarest looked past the navigator to where two figures approached the ship from across the field. "The captain and our passenger. When do we leave?"

"Before sunset."

"To where?"

Nimino's laugh was mocking. "Does it matter, my friend? To us, all worlds are much the same: places to reach and leave with the minimum of delay. But, if you are interested, we head for Argonilla."

They were five hours on their way when the engineer sent for Dumarest. He looked up from where he sat at his console, the winking lights of monitoring instruments throwing patches of transient color across his mottled face. On one side of his jaw a purple bruise spread high up his cheek.

"I'm sorry, Earl," he said. "I was drunk and didn't know what I was doing. You've got to believe that."

"All right," said Dumarest. "You were drunk. I believe you. Is that what you want?"

"I want you to understand. I felt sick when Lin told me what I'd tried to do. I mean that, Earl."

"Sure you do—until the next time." Dumarest stared down at the engineer, remembering the shattered tumbler, the stabbing points. "But if it happens again I'll kill you."

"You mean it," said Claude. "And I don't blame you. But it was the drink, not me." He blinked at the winking lights, touches of gaudy brightness illuminating his eyes. "It gets into me sometimes. The drink, I mean. It turns sour and then it's a sort of devil that's got to break loose. Anything can do it. One minute I'll be laughing and then, just like that, I'll be in a killing rage. That's why I'm not on the big ships," he confessed. "I was drinking on duty, the chief bawled me out and I smashed him up with a wrench. I didn't kill him but he was pretty bad. They gave me fifty lashes and threw me out. They marked my papers, too, and you can't get a berth on a decent vessel without them. Not on any ship as an engineer. Sheyan didn't seem to mind—with the little I get from my share he had no choice." He stood up from the console and held out his hand. "Can we forget it, Earl?"

The *Moray* was too small a vessel to harbor bad feelings.

Slowly Dumarest took the proffered hand. "All right," he said. "But remember what I told you."

"I'll remember." Claude winced as he touched his cheek. "I've got reason not to forget. You damn near broke my jaw."

"It hurts?"

"Like hell. Can you give me anything for it?"

"Sure," said Dumarest. "Can you come to my cabin?" Claude glanced at his instruments. "Not just yet. Give it to Lin to bring down. I want him to see the board when we reach supraspeed. The more experience he gets the better."

Dumarest found the steward in his cabin reading a worn copy of an engine manual and handed him the hypogun.

"This is for Claude," he said. "Take it down to him right away and give him one shot just over the bruise. Aim the nozzle within three inches and pull the trigger. Make certain you don't hit the eyes. Understand?"

Lin nodded, dropping the book as he rose. He stooped, picked it up, and carefully placed it on his bunk. "You and Claude all right now, Earl?"

"Yes."

"I'm glad. He's a good man, stupid when he hits the bottle but nice in a lot of other ways. Did I tell you he was teaching me how to be an engineer?"

"You did—and you'd better get that dope to him fast. We're close to supraspeed. Bring the hypogun back to me afterwards."

Dumarest was in his cabin when the steward returned. He sat on the edge of his bunk, a deck of cards in his hands, the cards intermeshing with a dry rustle as he manipulated the pack. Lin watched with interest; then, as he replaced the hypogun in its cabinet, said, "Why won't you let me join the game, Earl?"

"I told you: you'd lose."

The youngster was argumentative. "How can you be sure of that? Yalung said that the stakes needn't be high and he keeps asking me to join in. It wouldn't hurt to let me play, sometimes."

"You've got other things to do," said Dumarest. "Studying, for one. You won't become an officer if you waste your time and money."

"Please, Earl!"

Dumarest looked up and saw the young face, the eyes

now drained of their superficial hardness and filled with
the aching desire to know, to learn, to gain precious knowledge. To become adult in the shortest possible time. Once
he had felt exactly the same: impatient with the slow passage of the years and eager to gain experience so as to catch
up. He had gained it, learning the hard way, surviving his
mistakes and paying for his failures.

But how to pass on the accumulated knowledge of years?

Dumarest looked at the cards. It was a normal deck with
ace, lord, lady, jester, and ten to the deuce four times repeated in differentiating colors. Abruptly he riffled the deck
and slammed the cards on the table supporting the player.

"You want to gamble," he said. "We'll do just that. Make
a bet and cut—highest wins."

"That's a kid's game." Lin was disgusted. "A matter of
luck."

"You think so?" Dumarest picked up the deck and separated
three cards. "How about this, then? Find the jester." He
held two cards in his right hand, one in his left. The jester
was the lowest of the cards of his right. "See it?"

Lin nodded.

"Now bet." Dumarest moved his hands, the cards falling on the top of the player. "Which is the jester?"

"This one." Lin reached out to turn it over and winced
as Dumarest caught his wrist. "Earl! What the hell!"

"This isn't a game," said Dumarest flatly. "Where's your
money?"

Lin found coins and dropped them on the selected card.
Dumarest turned it over. "You lose. Try again."

Lin lost a second time, a third. At the eighth failure he
glared at Dumarest. "You're cheating!"

"No, how can I do that? The cards are all in front of you."
Dumarest picked them up and showed their faces to the
steward. "I'm outguessing you, that's all. You lack the experience to know what I'm doing. And you lack the experience to gamble with Yalung. He'll take you for all you've
got."

Lin was stubborn. "The luck could come my way."

"Luck has nothing to do with it," said Dumarest im-
patiently. "Not when you're playing with a professional
gambler. And there's something else." He scooped up the
money Lin had lost and heaped it to one side. From the
deck of cards he dealt two, one to either side of the coins.
"We're playing for the middle," he explained. "And I'm

betting one thousand that my card is higher than yours."

"A thousand!" Lin looked defeated. "I can't see you. I haven't that much money."

"So you lose." Dumarest picked up the coins. "You can't win against someone who can beat every bet you make. Understand?"

He didn't, of course, and he wouldn't grasp the point of the demonstration until he'd learned it the hard way. But Dumarest had done his part. Dropping the coins into Lin's hand he said to the relieved steward, "Stick to your books. Watch the play if you like, but remember—don't gamble out of your class."

Words, he thought as he followed Lin from the cabin, and ones which made good sense. But since when have the young ever listened to good advice? He would play and he would lose, and maybe he would learn after he had paid the price. But he wouldn't play on this ship and certainly not with Yalung.

Dumarest thought about the passenger as he made his way along the passage towards the control room. The yellow-faced man remained an enigma; the secret parts of his mind were bounded with layers of protection. Of only one thing was Dumarest certain: the man was addicted to gambling; he would play long past the time when other men would have become satiated. And he played shrewdly and well.

The door to the control room was unlocked. Dumarest pressed it open and stepped into a cool dimness where machines held a life of their own and instruments shone in soft reflections. To one side Nimino straightened from where he had stooped over a panel and raised a hand in warning.

"No noise," he said. "No sudden movement, Earl. It would be most unwise."

Dumarest followed the direction of his eyes. Slumped in the shielding confines of the big control chair, Sheyan's head was invisible beneath a mass of pulsing gray. It fitted like a cap, leaving only the mouth and nostrils clear.

"A symbiote from Elgart," explained the navigator quietly. "In return for a little blood it provides tranquilizing dreams. I remove it long before we are due to land."

"How long?"

"An hour. Sometimes more. What does it matter?"

A captain who was blind and deaf to any impending danger. It mattered!

"He cannot stand the sight of the stars," said Nimino,

guessing Dumarest's thoughts. "And he cannot leave the ship. He travels with fear as his constant companion. Call him a coward if you wish, but the fact remains."

"There are cures," said Dumarest. "Psychological manipulations."

"Perhaps, but not for Sheyan. His trouble cannot be cured, only accepted. For he is terrified of death and extinction. He will not accept the truths men have discovered: that one does not lead to the other. And without that conviction he is lost. The symbiote enables him to forget what he dare not face."

"He is mad," said Dumarest. "Insane."

"Can we really blame him? His life has been spent in the Web. How long can any man tread the edge of danger and remain wholly sane?" Nimino lifted his arm and pointed towards the screens. "Look at it, Earl. Try to imagine what you cannot see. The forces which are in continual imbalance as the stars fight for supremacy. That is why it is called the Web. Channels of relative safety run between the gravitational wells of stars and planets, slender lines like the filaments of a mass of gossamer. We have to follow them, threading our way with the aid of electronic sensors, balancing our speed and energy against external forces. And always, at any time, that delicate balance can be upset. Contraterrene matter exploding in a sun, a meshing of electromagnetic fields, solar flares and even the juxtaposition of worlds. And also there is the dust. Earl, no man who has not traversed the Web can appreciate its dangers."

IV

ARGONILLA WAS a cold, bleak, inhospitable world with snow thick on the landing field and sleet carried on the wind. Yalung took one look outside and retired to his cabin.

"There will be no stones of value here," he said positively. "And little of anything else."

Claude verified his prophecy. He came into the hold, blowing, his big frame muffled in shapeless garments. "They had a ship three days ago," he said disgustedly. "A trader bound for Thermyle. It took every decent pelt in the place."

Dumarest turned from where he tested the cargo restraints. "Do many ships call here bound for the terminal?"

"Hell, no. It was a wanderer dropping in on speculation to pick up anything that was going. The first ship to call in months and they beat us by three days. We would have done well."

"Trading iron for furs?"

"You're learning, Earl. This planet is short of heavy metal and we could have done a nice trade. Not now, though; there's no point in giving the stuff away. Sheyan's trying to get us something worth carrying." Claude shrugged. "I doubt if he'll find it."

The captain contracted for a load of hides to be brought to the ship and paid for when stowed. He left before half had arrived in order to avoid a coming storm. From Argonilla they went to Feen where they sold the hides and sonic recordings for cash, bought a quantity of crystallized extract of glandular secretions culled from a local life form, and gained a passenger.

Brother Angus of the Church of Universal Brotherhood was a small, elderly man with a wizened face and balding skull. He stood blinking in the bright light of the salon, diminutive in his robe of homespun, sandals on his bare feet, and the traditional begging bowl of chipped plastic in his hand.

Yalung, from where he sat at the table, said, "Greetings, brother. You seek charity?"

"To give is to acquire virtue," said the monk in a musical voice. He looked at the captain. "I understand that you are bound for Phane, brother. Is this so?"

"And if it is?"

"I beg your charity, brother, to give me a passage. I am willing to travel Low."

Sheyan frowned. In normal space monks were many, but hardly seen in the Web. The power of the Church in the small conglomeration of stars was negligible and it was safe to refuse. He tried to soften the blow.

"Phane is a hard world, brother, with little charity. I do not think you would be welcome."

"I do not ask for welcome, brother. Merely a place on which to set a church and to ease the hearts of men. The church," the monk added quickly, "is very small. A benediction light, some plastic sheeting and collapsible supports. I can carry the whole thing on my back."

Sheyan's frown deepened. "I would not care to take the

risk, brother. You talk of going to an inhospitable world."

Quietly the monk said, "Are there poor on Phane, brother?"

"There are poor everywhere," snapped the captain. "I am poor. Too poor to waste energy carrying unprofitable mass. I am sorry but I must refuse. The handler will guide you from the ship."

"Take him," said Dumarest.

"Will you pay his cost of a High passage?" Sheyan glared his anger. "From your share, perhaps? The profits we're making wouldn't even pay for his food."

"You're being foolish," insisted Dumarest. "The good will of the monks is worth having. It would be a wise investment to carry him to Phane. And we could use the luck he might bring us," he added. "The *Moray* can use all the luck it can get. Am I right, Nimino?"

"A holy man is worth more than a cargo of rotting hides," said the navigator. "Hides on which we would have made a profit had they been left behind. Earl is right, captain. It would be wisdom for you to gain virtue at this time."

Sheyan brooded then accepted defeat. "All right, have it your way. But I warn you, the cost of his passage will be deducted from our profits before I make the share."

Dumarest settled the monk in a cabin, carrying the collapsed bulk of the portable church from outside. Setting it down he looked at Brother Angus, who had sat on the bunk.

"You have been long in the Web, brother?"

"Many years. It is a hard place with hard men but I hope to have brought a little comfort into their bleak lives." The monk stretched, enjoying the warmth and relative comfort of the cabin. "You were kind to persuade your captain to give me passage. He seems to be an aggressive man."

"He is old and worried and afraid," said Dumarest, and added, casually, "In your travels, Brother, have you seen many cybers?"

Imperceptibly the monk stiffened. Between the Church and the Cyclan no love was lost, each regarding the other as would cat and dog. In the wizened face his eyes were shrewd as he answered the question.

"An odd thing to ask, brother, but the answer is no. There is little in the Web to attract those who wear the scarlet robe. No great houses or industrial combines. No ruling lords, managers, dictators, and chairmen. Most worlds have only one settlement and to sway their destiny would not be easy. And few could afford to purchase the service of the Cyclan. The advice of a cyber does not come cheap. You are new to the Web, brother?"

"Yes," said Dumarest.

"You have chosen a hard life with much danger and small reward."

Dumarest smiled. Few lives could be as hard and as unrewarding than that chosen by the monk. Living in poverty, surrounded by it, alleviating it as best they could, the servants of the Universal Church were to be found wherever men suffered most. In their portable churches they offered solace to tormented minds; the suppliants confessing their sins beneath the hypnotic glow of the benediction light, to be relieved of guilt and to suffer subjective penance before being given the bread of forgiveness.

And if most suppliants knelt as a prelude to obtaining the wafer of concentrate the monks did not mind. They considered it a fair exchange for the hypnotic conditioning they installed together with the penance. The command not to kill—the reason why Dumarest had never knelt before the glowing kaleidoscope of the benediction light.

At Phane they loaded synthetic fiber for Igar. From Igar to Landkis, to Oll, to Krieg: a scatter of insignificant worlds close to suns which burned like red hot embers in the dust. The *Moray* questing and probing as it rode from world to world, earning hardly enough to pay for the energy it used.

Claude brooded about it as he sat with the others, his nerves twitching with the need of alcohol. His supplies were exhausted; Krieg had been a temperate world without taverns. "We're going to end up owing money," he said. "A minus profit. A hell of a way for any trader to operate."

"The luck will change," said Lin. The steward had brought cups of basic from the salon. "You'll see. Nimino's working on it right now."

"Burning incense and mumbling incantations," said Claude.

"Praying to his gods and trying to bribe them to throw us a good cargo." He gulped half his meal and sat, scowling into the cup. A thread of vapor rose from it, the contents warmed by a heating element in the base. "How can a man with his brains be so stupid as to believe in such rubbish? And you're as bad," he added, glaring at Dumarest. "We should never have carried that monk. We were begging for trouble. The first rule of a trader is never to carry anything without profit. It's bad luck to break it."

"Now who's superstitious?" Dumarest sipped at his own cup. It contained enough energy to nourish a spaceman for a day and it was all they had been eating since entering the Web. "Luck has nothing to do with it. Sheyan moves on too fast. He should wait until the news of the *Moray*'s arrival has had time to spread. My guess is that we are missing cargoes because we're gone before they can be delivered."

"No," said Claude. "It doesn't work like that. On other worlds, perhaps, but not in the Web. Cargoes are assembled and waiting for the first ship to arrive. We've been unlucky. On Argonilla and Landkis we arrived just too late. Oll had been stripped a week before we got there." He drank again, frowning. "Let's hope we have better luck on Candara."

Candara was an ancient world, great seas lapping a solitary land mass composed of low hills, boulders, leached and inferior soil. Straggling vines, olives, and other cultivated crops surrounded the settlement with beasts grazing beyond on rough foliage. The foothills were crusted with trees, shining a dull brown in the light of a somber sun.

"Candara," said Nimino as he stood beside Dumarest in the open port. "Sheol would have been a better name. Look at it, Earl. Who do you think would ever choose to settle here?"

Dumarest could guess. The followers of a minor sect turning their backs on civilized comfort for the sake of imagined spiritual reward. Masochists who took a delight in physical hardship. Unfortunates who had had no choice. The dispossessed glad of any world to call their own.

"You were right the first time," said Nimino. "They are a hard people following a hard path towards the Ultimate. They may be right, but I would not like to emulate them." He lifted an arm, pointing. "You see that building? The one with the tower and walls of massive stone? That is their temple. I have seen the inside, a gloomy place devoid of color, the very air depresses with thoughts of the tomb."

"Do they have wine?" Dumarest was thinking of the engineer.

"Ceremonial vintage only. Twice a year they release their emotions in a great feast. They have the best food available and wallow in wine. There is singing and dancing and marriages take place. Fighting, too, as old scores are paid. For three days they enjoy civilized dissipation and then, ashamed, they spend the next six months in hard work and repentance." Nimino shook his head. "An odd way to live and yet they must find it to their liking. Never yet have we had anyone asking for passage."

"Perhaps they can't afford it."

"Or perhaps they are afraid to step outside their own narrow world," said the navigator shrewdly. "There is a comfort in recognized boundaries." He turned as Lin called from beyond the hold. "Sheyan is waiting for me to accompany him to the chief elder. Why don't you join us?"

"And Claude?"

"He remains behind. The last time we were here he drank too deeply of the guest-offering. Need I say more?"

Two men waited with the captain. They were stern, middle-aged, dressed in plain garments of undyed wool; their hair long and held by a fillet of hammered steel. Each carried a staff as tall as himself and as thick as three fingers. Their faces were deeply scored and devoid of humor. The honor guard, thought Dumarest, or the escort to restrict the contaminating influence of the visitors. He fell into step behind the captain as they led the way towards a squat building built of stone and roofed with shells.

Inside was a long table, benches, and a rack to hold clothing. All were roughly made of wood; the marks of the tools clearly visible. The floor was of tamped dirt polished until it shone like lambent glass. As they entered, the chief elder rose from the head of the table. He could have been the father of the guards.

"I am Herkam, the chief elder," he intoned. "I bid you welcome."

"I am Sheyan, captain of the *Moray*. These men are of my crew." Sheyan gestured, naming them. "I thank you for your welcome. Your hospitality will not be abused."

It was a ritual and belonged to the setting. An event to break the monotony and to add to the prestige of the chief elder. Dumarest sat when bidden and shared in the guest-offering of cakes and wine. The cakes were small, made of rough-ground flour with a nutty consistency and surprisingly sweet. The wine was better than he had anticipated.

"The law of hospitality," whispered Nimino at his side. "Now we cannot be injured or detained."

The formalities dispensed with, the business then commenced. Prepared skins of giant fish, soft and with a scaled gleam, ornaments of carven bone, unusual shells, giant crystals which sang when struck, and vials of oil which formed the base of costly perfume began to pile on the table. They were samples from the stocks held in the warehouse. Sheyan's hands quivered a little as he inspected them.

"The goods are of fine quality," he admitted. "I have seen better, but these are good. Yet, as good as they are, the market for such things is small. Have you nothing else?"

Necklets of amber, pieces of stone striated with luminous color, fronds of dried weed which gave off aromatic perfumes when burned joined the other goods on the table.

Dumarest watched as the captain examined them. Already he knew what really interested the man, the vials of costly oil, his other actions were to cover his real object which was to obtain the oils at the lowest possible price. But he was too transparent. Either the run of bad luck had affected his nerves or his eagerness had numbed his caution.

"You have seen what we have to offer," said the chief elder. Sunken in the seams of his harsh face his eyes never left the captain's. "What have you to offer in exchange?"

"Iron," said Sheyan. "Implements to work the soil."

"Our religion forbids us to use the things of the Evil One," said Herkam sternly. "We have tools of wood and shell and stone. Nature's free gifts to us, her children. These things we can make at any time."

Dumarest said, "And fishhooks?"

The shrewd eyes flickered as Herkam looked down the table. "You have such things?"

"Of many sizes," said Dumarest, ignoring the captain's glare. "Together with fine chains and gaffs of steel."

"We may see them?"

"Tomorrow." Dumarest didn't look at the captain. "Now, if we have your leave to depart, we will begin unstacking our cargo."

Sheyan remained silent while within earshot of the guards, but once back in the privacy of the *Moray*, he exploded.

"What the hell do you think you're doing? I gave you leave to come and watch—not to take over. You've ruined a good trade. A ship could land at any time and snatch it from under our noses."

"A ship carrying fishhooks?"

"What's that got to do with it?"

44

"Everything." Dumarest was curt. "I suggest that you use your mouth less and your eyes more. This is a world almost wholly composed of ocean. You saw those skins and sea products. How do you think they catch such big fish?"

"With nets," said Nimino. "And spears. I've seen them."

"Nets that are easy to break and hard to mend. With spears made of wood and stone and shell. You heard the chief elder. How strong do you think a spear like that is against what must live in the ocean?" Dumarest looked from one to the other. "You don't know," he said. "You've never had to fish for your food. I have and, believe me, there's nothing quite so hard to make as a strong fishhook if you can't use metal. Chains, too, in order to prevent the catch from biting through the line. And gaffs so that you can hook it aboard. Supply what I promised and you'll have no trouble getting your oil."

Sheyan bridled. "How did you know that was what I wanted?"

"I knew," said Dumarest. "And Herkam knew also. If you take my advice you'll ask for everything else but the oil. Set the price of the hooks ridiculously high in terms of skins and amber, weed and crystals; a thousand times its own weight. The chains and gaffs a little less, they can do without those if they have to. But they can't do without the hooks."

"He makes sense, captain," said Nimino. "Don't forget, Earl is a gambler, he knows how to bluff."

"How to lie, you mean," snapped Sheyan. "How can we trade what we haven't got?"

"We'll get it," said Dumarest. "We'll make it. There are tools in the engine room and laser torches to cut and fuse and use as a forge. And we have rods of iron as well as the rest of the stuff. With five of us working full time we'll be able to make what we need."

"By tomorrow?" Regretfully Nimino shook his head. "It's a good plan, Earl, but we can't do it in the time. We haven't the experience and we'll be slow. We simply haven't the time to both learn and manufacture."

"Yes we have," said Dumarest. "We'll use slowtime."

Herkam slowly lifted the length of chain and let it fall, link by link, to the surface of the table. It was well-made: half-inch circles linked and welded tight. The gaffs were rougher, adapted from hoes cut and shaped and sharpened

into curved tines. The hooks were cruder still, the un-
polished metal showing signs of tools and tempering, but
they were viciously barbed with an eye for the leader and
filed to a needle point.

"These items are of worth," said the chief elder slowly.
"Our young men die too often while fishing the waters, falling prey to the beasts that live in the ocean; yet our land
is poor and we need the meat of the sea. Even so I cannot
take them. All night I have wrestled in prayer, seeking
guidance from the All Powerful, and counsel from the
vaults of the dead; they remained silent yet I know what
must be done. We cannot use the fabrications of the Evil
One."

"The iron used was that received from the skies," said
Sheyan quickly. Primed by Dumarest he was ready to bluff,
by Nimino ready to lie and to turn the religion of the elder
to his own ends. "As such surely it is a natural thing? As
natural as stone and wood and shell. Meteors, by their nature,
cannot be from the domain of the Evil One."

Herkam nodded, willing to be convinced, and Dumarest
gained the impression that he had raised the objection merely in order to lower the price.

"You make a point, captain. One which has to be gravely
considered. Let us do so over a glass of wine."

Was the old man delaying, perhaps hoping for the arrival
of another trader? Dumarest doubted it. The last time the
Moray had called it had carried biological fertilizers, wool,
strains of mutated yeast, seeds and artifacts of iron-hard
wood. All natural things according to the dogma of the
Candarians. Sheyan had never guessed that his load of iron
might prove worthless.

Dumarest swallowed his wine, feeling the rich liquid ease
some of the fatigue which ached his bones. He looked at
his hands, bruised and discolored with pressure and strain.
Slowtime was a dangerous drug to use on a wakeful man.
It accelerated the metabolism and slowed normal time to a
fortieth of its normal passing. A man so drugged would
move forty times as fast, do forty times as much. But care
had to be taken. Flesh and bone could not stand the shattering impact of a normal blow. The touch had to be gentle,
the movements under constant control. He had the knack
and so did Nimino. They had used the drug while the others
did the rough work. Moving, gulping down pints of basic to

replenish lost energy, sleeping to wake and eat and work and eat again.

Always eating to ward off starvation, getting hurt and bruised, doing the labor of forty times their number.

Dumarest blinked and drank a little more wine. Later he would sleep and restore the strength he had expended. Now he wanted to follow the progress of the trading.

It was going well. Sheyan, recovered from his initial over-eagerness, confident that he now had what the chief elder wanted, was pressing a hard bargain.

"The weed is bulky," he said. "My hold would barely take the worth of a dozen hooks. The skins are better and the crystals even more so, yet still they have bulk and my hold is small."

"And the oil?" Herkam pushed forward a container. It was of baked clay sealed with wax. "This would take but little room."

"True." Deliberately Sheyan broke the seal and poured some of the contents into the hollow of his palm. He rubbed his hands, smelled, frowned, smelled again. "An extract from a fish?"

"From the giant clams which live deep in the water. They have a gland which can be milked. From the oil can be made a costly perfume."

Nimino smiled and whispered, "Do you think Sheyan is overacting, Earl? Maybe you'd better end the bargain before he talks us all out of a profit."

"He's doing well." Dumarest reached out and helped himself to more wine. The container was a gourd bright with inset shells and had probably taken some woman a year to make. "This is no time to interfere."

Sheyan slammed his hand hard on the table. "Done! The oil, the crystals, some amber and skins in the ratio agreed on. In return we give the hooks chains and gaffs. Can we load immediately?"

"First we must drink to seal the bargain." The haggling done the chief elder could afford to relax a little. "You find our wine palatable?"

"It is a rare vintage." Sheyan, too, had relaxed. He had driven a hard bargain and had cause to be satisfied. "A veritable gift of nature."

"And, as such, not to be swilled as the food of swine," said the chief elder sternly. "Mother Nature has given us the grape to be used for the comfort of guests and the libation of sacrifice." He sipped at his glass. "And now, captain, there is a service I must ask you to perform."

Sheyan narrowed his eyes. "And that is?"

"A matter of dissension which needs to be settled."

"A trial?"

"That and perhaps more. I beg your indulgence for this imposition on a guest, but the matter must be settled immediately. You will form a tribunal?"

"Of course." Sheyan gestured towards Dumarest and Nimino. "These two officers will accompany me. When will you need us?"

"Two hours after sunset, captain. I shall send men to escort you to the meeting house."

"So late?" The captain's voice echoed his displeasure. "I could be loaded and ready to leave in an hour. Time is money to a trader."

"Two hours after sunset," repeated the chief elder firmly. "It will be dark and the workers will be in from the fields and the sea. You may load, captain, everything but the oil. That we shall deliver to you after the trial."

V

NIGHT CAME with a thin wind gusting from the sea, a mist of cloud hiding the stars and intensifying the darkness. Men with torches came to escort the tribunal, their faces hard and solemn in the guttering light. Nimino's voice was low as he walked beside Dumarest, both men three paces behind the captain.

"We get this from time to time. As traders we're considered to be impartial and when a hard decision has to be made we are asked to give it. That way no one has any reason to hold a grudge. A lot of these worlds have a tribal culture or large families locked in a struggle for power. A vendetta would ruin them and most are too proud or too wary to submit to the judgment of other residents." Nimino stumbled as his foot caught an obstruction and he grabbed at Dumarest's arm to save himself from falling. "I just hope that we don't have to execute anyone."

The meeting house was a long, low-roofed structure built of logs caulked with clay, lit by flaring torches, and hung with a clutter of various trophies. Benches accommodated the audience, the sour reek of their bodies rising to blend with the resinous smell of the torches, the odor of damp soil.

Dumarest studied them as he took his seat on the raised platform occupying one end of the hall. They wore either rough jerkins and trousers made of treated fish skins or somber garments of wool. The fishers and farmers, he decided; but aside from their clothes they seemed all cast from the same mold. Like the elderly guards, their faces were set in fanatical lines as if to laugh was to commit a sin. Hair was long and held back with fillets of skin or leather; those of hammered steel being obviously a badge of authority. There were no young women present but a double row of matrons, shapeless in voluminous dresses, sat at the extreme rear.

Nimino leaned towards Dumarest and said quietly, "Look at their eyes, Earl. Have you ever seen such an expression before?"

It was the blood-lust glare inherent to mobs and to those anticipating blood and pain. He had seen it a hundred times in the eyes of watchers clustered around a ring where men fought with ten-inch blades. At his side Sheyan moved restlessly on the hard wooden chair.

"Why the delay?" he said to the chief elder. "We are assembled, where is the prisoner?"

There was a stir at the far end of the hall. A dozen men, guards, hard-faced and no longer young, marched forward with someone in their midst. They halted before the raised platform and stepped back, their staves swinging horizontal before them to form a barrier. Isolated in the clear space before the platform, a girl looked coolly at the tribunal.

"By God," she said. "Men. Real men at last!"

"Silence!" Herkam's voice was harsh with anger. "There will be no blasphemy. Guards! If the woman Lallia speaks so again you will strike her down!"

Nimino drew in his breath with an audible hiss. "By the sacred mantras of the Dedla Vhal," he said. "That is a woman!"

She was tall, with a mane of lustrous black hair which swept from a high forehead and rested on her left shoulder. Beneath a rough dress of undyed wool the curves of her body strained under the fabric. Her skin was white, arms and feet bare, the long column of her throat unadorned. The long-lashed eyes were bold, challenging, and the full lips held a wealth of sensuous passion.

Herkam looked at Sheyan, at the others of the tribunal. "This is the one on whom you must pass judgment," he said. "She came to us several months ago from a ship which called here. We gave her the guest offering of food and wine and accepted the stranger within our gates. In return she has sowed dissension, turning brother against brother, mocking our sacred ways and filling the young men with thoughts of evil. We gave her work among the women and she dazzled their minds with tales of orgies, dancing, fine raiment, and decadent living. We put her to work alone and then had to set guards to keep the young men away from the enticement of her body."

"A moment." Sheyan lifted his hand. "What is the charge against her?"

"That of witchcraft! Of consorting with the Evil One!"

"The evidence?"

It was as Dumarest expected; a list of petty incidents inconsequential in themselves, but in this in-bred, neurotic community, swollen to grotesque proportions. A woman had pricked her thumb while cleaning fish skins, the resultant infection was wholly due to the accused's evil eye. A young man had died while fishing—a spell must have been laid on his spear so that it broke at a critical time. Crops had withered after she had walked among them. A baby had sickened after she had spoken to it.

Dumarest looked at the chief elder during the interminable list of complaints and accusations. Herkam was no fool and must know the real value of what was being said. Lallia was guilty of arousing nothing more than jealously and resentment among the women, desire and frustration among the men. And yet, in such a community, such emotions were dangerous. He began to understand why the case had been given to outsiders to judge.

"This is a bad one, Earl." Nimino's voice was barely a whisper. "We're dealing with fanaticism and aberrated fears —an ugly combination."

It was more than that. Dumarest leaned back, watching the faces of the girl, the men and women seated on the benches. Herkam was playing a shrewd game of politics and playing it well. There would be factions for and against the girl. Young men of high family would be enamored of her beauty, each snarling like a dog over a favored bone, each determined that if he could not win the prize then it should fall to no other. The women would be banded in a common determination to bring her down. Herkam would be trying to both maintain the peace and his own authority.

And shortly would come the time of festival when the wine flowed and old scores were settled. A time of unleashed passion and explosive violence. In such an atmosphere the girl would be a match to tinder and, no matter what happened, the chief elder would be held to blame.

Dumarest leaned forward as the accusations ceased and said to Sheyan. "Let us hear from the girl herself."

"There's no need," the captain was sharp. "She'd deny everything, what else would you expect?"

"He's right, Earl." Nimino joined the low conversation. "We're not dealing with justice here. The girl is innocent, of course, but we daren't say so. They wouldn't accept it. They want her to be found guilty and destroyed. Herkam wants that, too, but he doesn't want her blood on his hands." The navigator frowned, thinking. "We could take her with us but I doubt if they would let her go. They have to be proved right and they want to see her suffer."

"We could execute her," said Sheyan. "At least that would be quick."

"No," said Dumarest.

"What else?" The captain's face was bunched, knotted with anger. "Do you want her to be burned? Or have you got some crazy idea of rescuing her? If you have forget it. We're three against an entire community and we wouldn't even get out of this hall. And we'd lose the oil," he added. "Unless we play this Herkam's way he won't release it."

"The oil," said Dumarest tightly. "Is that all you're thinking about?"

"I'm thinking of the ship, the crew, your share and mine. Do you think I intend to throw away the best trade I've ever made for the sake of some stupid slut? Look at her!" Sheyan gestured to where Lallia stood, waiting. "A cheap harlot who got herself dumped. Well, to hell with her! I'm no wet nurse to aid the fallen. She's got herself into a mess and she can't expect us to lose our profit to get her out. I say we return a verdict of guilty."

"No," said Dumarest again. "She's innocent and we all know it."

"What's that got to do with it?" Sheyan looked at his hands, they were trembling. "Don't push it, handler," he said harshly. "I don't like doing this but it has to be done. We won't get that oil unless we act smart—and I intend getting that oil. A majority vote will do it. Nimino?"

The navigator hesitated. "She is very beautiful. To destroy such beauty would be a crime."

"Are you turning soft on me?"

"No, captain, but there could be another way. Do you object to taking her with us?"

"As long as we get the oil—no."

"And you, Earl? Will you help?"

Dumarest was wary. "What have you got in mind?"

"A trick," said Nimino. "An appeal to their religious convictions. It is the only chance the woman has."

The hall fell silent as Nimino rose to his feet, soft whispers dying to be replaced by a straining expectancy. In the guttering torchlight eyes gleamed savage, feral: the eyes of animals rather than those of men. From where he stood to one side, the chief elder stepped towards the tribunal.

"Have you reached your verdict?"

"We have." The navigator's voice rolled with the power of an incantation. "It is the verdict of us all."

"And that is?"

Deliberately Nimino took his time before answering, letting the silence lengthen to obtain dramatic effect. He was a good actor, thought Dumarest, and was putting to use the things he had learned from attending numerous religious ceremonies. Casually he glanced at the woman. Lallia stood, tense, white teeth gnawing at her lower lip. Her eyes, no longer bold, held a shadow of worry. The tribunal had taken too long, there had been too much discussion, and she was cynical in her knowledge of the ways of men. Dumarest caught the slight tension of muscles beneath the fabric of her dress, the tensing of thighs and stomach, the unconscious reaction of a person who readied herself for struggle or flight.

But there was nowhere to run and she would not have to fight.

"Your verdict?" Herkam's nerve had snapped and he spoke to break the tension. "What is your decision?"

"That the woman face trial by combat!"

It was totally unexpected. The chief elder's face went blank as he tried to grasp the implications and Nimino spoke again, quickly, before he could protest.

"We have traveled many worlds and have seen the manifestations of the All Powerful in many guises. And, too, we have seen the malicious designs of the Evil One. Who can gauge the extent of his cunning? Who can deny that they are proof against his insidious evil? This woman has been accused of witchcraft and it may well be that she is guilty. If so then she must be put to death for it is an abomination that such as she be allowed to live. But if she has been wrongly accused, what then?"

"She is a witch!"

"Kill her!"

"Slay the thing of evil!"

The voices poured from where the double row of matrons sat at the rear of the hall. Others, less coherent, came from the assembled men. Several sprang to their feet, arms waving, feet stamping the dirt of the floor.

"Hold!" The chief elder signaled to the guards and heavy staves lifted and fell as they beat the young men back into their places. "There will be silence in this place. We deal with a human life and that is not a thing to be treated without due solemnity." He turned to where Nimino stood. "Explain."

"The charge of witchcraft is one easy to make and hard to refute," continued the navigator. "It could be that the All Powerful has reached forth to place the truth on the lips of those who accuse—or it could be that the Evil One seeks to rend the hearts of those same accusers by causing them to bear false witness. If that should be the case, and if the accused should die because of it, then woe to the people of Candara." His voice deepened, echoed with rolling thunder. "They shall die and perish to be blown away by the wind. Their crops shall fail and their cattle abort and the beasts of the sea shall withhold their meat. Demons shall come to torment the night with ceaseless dreams and all shall perish to become as dust in the wind. For the All Powerful will not extend the wing of protection to those who are seduced by the Evil One. There will be no peace, no comfort, brother shall turn against brother and man shall turn against wife. All, all will be totally lost and pass as if they had never been. This I prophesy!"

Herkam frowned; he had no liking for anyone but himself making such prophecies, especially not visiting traders. And things were not going as he had planned. He had expected a quick verdict of guilty in which case the woman could have been disposed of and the incident forgotten.

He said sharply, "We know full well the might of the All Powerful. What does your verdict imply?"

Nimino smiled, white teeth flashing in the torchlight. "The woman denies being a witch," he said. "We have decided that the matter be judged by a Higher Power. If her champion falls then she is proven guilty. If not, then she must be allowed to depart in peace."

The thing had its possibilities. The chief elder pondered them, conscious of the watchful eyes in the hall, the air of anticipation. A fight would provide the needed spectacle, the necessary blood and, in the remote event of the woman's champion winning, he would be able to castigate those who had made the accusations. In either case he would be rid of the troublemaker. But it would be best if the woman did not win.

He said, "Who is the woman's champion?"

Dumarest rose. "I am."

Herkam felt a glow of inner satisfaction. A trader. One who, by the nature of his employment, must of necessity lack the strength of a manual worker.

"I bow to your verdict," he said sonorously. And then, to the guards, said, "Find Gilliam and bring him here."

The man was an atavar, a monster, a mutated freak spawned from radiation-distorted genes. Seven feet tall, his shoulders and arms heavy with ridged and knotted muscle, his legs as thick and as strong as the boles of gnarled trees, he lumbered from the rear of the hall and stood blinking in the cleared space before the platform. Matted hair fell to just above his deep-set eyes. Bare feet, callused and scarred, toed the ground. His hands clenched as a voice rumbled from the depths of his chest.

"You want Gilliam, chief elder?"

"I want you to fight." Herkam pointed towards Dumarest. "This is the man."

"To kill?"

"To kill." Herkam gestured at the guards. "Take him and prepare him for battle."

"Earl, I'm sorry." Nimino sucked in his breath. "I didn't know. I thought they would use one of the guards. You're fast and could have taken any of them without trouble. Who would have guessed they had a monster like that?"

"Win or lose I want that oil." Sheyan's face was furrowed with worry. "If you fall, Dumarest, I'm sorry; but it will be just too bad. There's nothing we can do to help you. You go and the girl goes with you."

Dumarest looked to where she stood, the full lips blood-less now, her eyes like those of a trapped beast. The hands at her sides were clenched, the knuckles showing white beneath the skin. She turned and caught his eyes, her own following him as he stepped from the platform and moved towards her.

"Mister," she said flatly, "I thank you for what you're try-ing to do, but you haven't got a chance. That freak can't be stopped."

"You want me to pull out?"

"No." Her voice was resonant, musical beneath the harsh-ness of strain. "This way I've got a slim chance," she ad-mitted. "The other way I've got none at all. These crazy people want my blood and if you quit they'll get it." She shivered a little. "Look at them! Animals! And Gilliam's the worst. He's an idiot, solid bone and muscle with the intel-ligence of a five-year-old. They use him to haul up the boats and do all the heavy stuff. Sometimes he goes insane and then they have to catch him in nets and tie him down. As a reward they let him slaughter the cattle. He thinks it's fun."

Dumarest looked to where men clustered around the giant. They were stripping him, coating him with oil, fastening a loincloth of leather around his hips. Dwarfed by his stature the chief elder stood to one side, hands lifted, lips moving as he called a blessing down on the champion of the people.

Nimino came to stand beside the girl and Dumarest.

"You'd better get ready, Earl," he said, his voice reflecting his worry. "Is there anything I can do?"

"Fetch him a laser," said Lallia. "That or a score of men to help him out."

The navigator ignored the comment. "Well, Earl?"

"No." Dumarest flexed his toes in his shoes, his shoulders beneath the material of his uniform. The plastic was firm and would give some protection against the claws of his opponent. "Do we fight bare-handed?"

A guard came forward and handed him a stave. It was a plain length of wood, six feet long and two inches thick; both ends were bound with leather. Nimino stepped back, pulling the girl with him as Gilliam moved to the center of the open space.

"I kill," he said. And rushed forward.

Dumarest ducked and felt the wind brush his hair, the drone of the staff's passing sounding like a deep-toned bee. Immediately he sprang aside as Gilliam, turning with amazing speed, again lashed out with the staff. He held it in one great hand, wielding it as a boy would a stick, lashing with the full power of his arms and shoulders at the darting figure in the cleared space.

"Good luck, Earl!" called Nimino.

"Kill him, Earl!" said the girl.

Dumarest ignored the encouragement as he warily darted from the attacks of his opponent. He held his own staff horizontal before him, each hand a third of the way from either end, ready to parry or strike as the opportunity presented itself. The weapon was clumsy, awkward to handle, needing much practice before a man could become proficient in its use. Had Gilliam used it properly Dumarest knew that he would already be dead.

He ducked again, darted to one side, sprang back as a vicious downswing caused the air to strike his eyeballs. It was useless to attempt to tire his opponent, those great muscles would house inexhaustible energy and, too, they protected the bone beneath. Letting trained reflexes govern his evading movements Dumarest studied the weak points against which he must aim his attack: the groin, joints, eyes, and throat. The groin presented too small a target and was protected by the swell of thighs and the ridged muscle of the belly. A successful attack could win the contest but the chances were against it being successful. The deep-set eyes were set with ridges of overhanging bone; the spade of the chin lowered over the vulnerable throat. The elbows were awkward to get at.

Only one thing was really in his favor: the limited intelligence of the giant. Gilliam had been given a staff and told to kill his opponent. He tried to do it with the staff alone instead of adding the weapon to his natural armory. Also he was using it as a saber—and any man armed with a quarterstaff could beat a swordsman.

If he were skilled with its use.

If the swordsman had normal strength.

Again the giant swung his staff through the air. Dumarest ducked, straightened, and saw the length of wood sweeping in a backhand slash towards his skull. Desperately he threw up his own staff, the wood meeting with a vicious crack, the force of the interrupted blow knocking his own weapon hard against the side of his head. Dazed, Dumarest fell to the ground, rolling frantically as the staff whined down towards him, the end gouging deep as he sprang to his feet.

"Kill!" gloated the giant. "I kill!"

Dumarest tensed as the giant reared back, the staff lifted high. His hands shifted as he altered his grip on his own weapon. Should Gilliam sweep his staff downwards in a cutting blow then he must spring to one side and slam the end of his own pole directly into one of the eyes. If he should try a sidewise swing then he must duck and strike before the giant could recover his balance.

Air droned as the staff swept towards him.

Dumarest crouched, straightened, and struck at the side of the giant's face, the end of his staff smashing against the prominent ridge of bone protecting the eye. Immediately Gilliam turned, staff whining in a backhand blow. Dumarest sprang from it, throwing himself behind the giant's back, poising himself with the staff held by the end in both hands, the tip well beyond his shoulder. As the giant, baffled, turned again to find his elusive opponent, Dumarest sprang forward, the staff a blur as he sent the length of wood hard against the exposed kneecap. There was a dull crack of yielding bone and Gilliam staggered, his face distorting in pain.

"Hurt," he mumbled. "Hurt!"

Dumarest struck again, viciously, using the full strength of back and shoulders. Again the staff cracked against the broken kneecap. As it did he threw himself backward in a complete somersault, landing just beyond the reach of the giant's staff.

Gilliam sprang after him. Sprang and fell as his shattered knee refused to carry his enormous weight. As he crashed to the ground Dumarest leaped forward, staff lifted high above his head, smashing it down at the base of the muscular neck. Twice he struck. At the third blow the staff cracked and fell apart. Chest heaving, the broken end of the staff held sword-fashion in his right hand, Dumarest stepped towards the fallen giant.

Nimino caught his arm as he went to stab the splintered end into the corded throat.

"That's enough, Earl! Earl, damn you, that's enough! You've won!"

Dumarest drew air deep into his lungs and looked at the shattered staff in his hand. "He's dead?"

"Stone cold. You snapped his neck."

"Good." Dumarest lifted a hand and touched a wetness on his head. One of the giant's wild blows must have torn his scalp. He looked at the blood on his hand. How close had death been then? Quietly he said, "So I've won. Now get us out of here. All of us. The girl as well."

"And the oil," said Sheyan as he joined the group. "Don't forget the oil."

VI

"PEARLS," SAID YALUNG. He tilted his cupped hand, the salon light filling his palm with nacreous beauty. "They are fine but . . ." Regretfully he shook his head. "On every world there are seas and in every sea there are bivalves. They are very pretty, my dear, but I'm afraid of very little value."

"These are special," said Lallia. "And you know it."

She sat on the edge of the table, long bare legs swinging beneath the hem of an iridescent dress made of finely tanned fish skin. Three hours from Candara, bathed, her lustrous black hair piled in thick coils above her head, she had doubled her beauty.

And her boldness, thought Dumarest. He sat beside her, facing the dealer in precious stones, feeling the ache of fatigue gnaw at his bones. The fight had drained the last of his strength.

"They are special," admitted Yalung after a moment. "To you, no doubt, they are very special. To others, my dear, they are merely pearls. How did you get them from their owners?"

Lallia smiled. "I own them. They were given to me by love-sick fools. I hid them in a place only my lover shall find." Her hand reached out, the slim fingers running through Dumarest's hair.

"And the dress?" Yalung was curious.

"I wore it beneath that stinking woolen thing they made me put on. The men weren't allowed to touch me and the old biddies were satisfied as long as I didn't dazzle their men. Men!" She snorted her contempt. "Blind fools who lived in terror of imagined perils to come. The old ones were the worst, coming to me with the excuse they wanted to save me from eternal damnation. When that didn't work they tried to buy what they wanted. I took what they gave and laughed in their faces. The fools!"

"You were the fool," said Dumarest flatly. "Didn't you even think of the dangers you ran?"

"I thought a ship would come," she admitted. "I hoped every day that a trader would call. When it did I didn't even see it. They had me locked away in the dark. God, you'll never know how relieved I was to see some real men again!"

Again she reached out to caress Dumarest's hair.

"Real men," she murmured. "And one of them a very real man indeed. Tell me, lover, am I to your liking?"

"He fought for you," said Yalung. "He could have died for you. Would a man do that for someone he cared nothing about?"

"I want him to say it," she said and then, as Dumarest remained silent, "well, perhaps later. What will you give for the pearls, dealer? And don't think I'm some ignorant fool who doesn't know their real worth."

"I will give you the cost of a High passage," said Yalung. "More I cannot give."

"Then forget it." Reaching out she took the pearls from the yellow palm. "The captain will give me more than that. More than you think, perhaps." She smiled at Dumarest, her face radiant. "Can you guess, lover, at what I mean?"

Again Dumarest remained silent. Yalung said, "Tell me, girl, how did you come to be on Candara?"

"I wanted to travel the Web so I entered into a ship-marriage with an engineer. I didn't know that he rode a commune ship and he didn't tell me until we were well on our way. They share everything they own and I refused to be shared. So, when we hit Candara, they kicked me out." She laughed, remembering. "They didn't do any trade, though. I told the chief man that they practiced abominable rites and he believed me. So they went off empty-handed."

Dumarest looked at the long length of her naked thigh. "And before that?"

"You're interested, lover?" Her teeth were white against the red of her mouth. "Before that I worked in a carnival. Reading palms, that sort of thing. And before that I—"

"You read palms?" Yalung interrupted, his smile bland. "Surely not."

"I don't lie, dealer. Give me your paw and I'll tell you things." She reached out for the yellow hand as Yalung snatched it away. "No? Scared, maybe?"

"Cautious," he said, smiling. "Why don't you read the hand of our friend here?"

"Why not?" Lallia again ran her fingers through Dumarest's hair. They were gentle, caressing. "Give me your hand, Earl." She studied it, brooding, the tips of her slender fingers tracing lines, hesitating from time to time, the touch as gentle as the impact of butterflies. "A strange hand," she murmured. "One not easy to read. There is a sense of power and a mystery hard to unravel. You have lived close to violence for a long time now, lover. You have traveled far and will travel further. You have loved and lost, and you will love again. And you have a great enemy." She sucked in her breath. "Earl! I see danger!"

"A carnival trick!" He jerked his hand away with sudden irritation. "Shall I read your palm?" He caught her hand and, without looking at the mesh of lines, said, "You have ambition. You have dreams and are never long content. You have known many men and many worlds and there are those who have reason to hate your name. You are greedy and selfish and will come to a bad end. Is that enough or do you want more?"

"You—"

He caught her wrist as she swung her hand at his cheek.

"Don't, you're hurting me!" Her eyes widened as she looked into his face. "Earl! Don't look at me like that! Don't make me feel so unclean!"

He dropped her hand, fighting his sudden, inexplicable anger. Who was he to judge? Like himself she was a traveler making out as best she could. And if she used her woman's wiles to get her way, was that any different to him using his natural speed and acquired skill? Was it worse to hurt a man's pride than to gash his body with blades?

"I'm sorry, Lallia," he said. "I'm tired and spoke without thinking. Please forget it."

"I'm sorry too, Earl. Sorry that we didn't meet years ago. Things could have been so different if we had." She dropped her right hand to his left, squeezed, her fingers tight against his ring. "Earl!"

"What is it?" He stared into her face. It was pale, beaded with perspiration, suddenly haggard with lines of strain. "Lallia!"

"Death," she muttered. "And pain. So much pain. And a hopeless longing. Oh, such a hopeless longing!"

And then, abruptly, she collapsed, falling to lie sprawled on the table, naked arms and legs white against the iridescence of her dress, the dingy plastic of the surface.

Nimino rubbed the side of his chin with one slender finger and looked thoughtfully down at the girl on the bunk. "A sensitive," he said wonderingly. "Who would have suspected it?"

"Are you sure?" Dumarest had carried the girl into his cabin and now stood beside the navigator.

"I'm sure. She has all the characteristic symptoms of one who has suffered a severe psychic shock. I have seen it many times before." Nimino leaned forward and lifted one eyelid exposing the white ball of the eye. "You see? And feel the skin, cold and clammy when it should be warm and dry. The pulse, too—there can be no mistake."

Dumarest stared curiously at the girl. She lay at full length, the mass of her hair, which had become unbound, a midnight halo around the paleness of her face. The long curves of arms and legs were filled with the clean lines of developed muscle covered with scanty fat. The breasts were full and proud, the stomach flat, the hips melting into rounded buttocks. A courtesan, he thought, the typical body of a woman of pleasure, all warmth and smoothness and femininity.

And yet—a sensitive?

He had met them before, the sports of mutated genes, the products of intense inbreeding. Always they had paid for their talent. Sometimes with physical weakness or irregular development of body or mind. But always they had paid. Lallia?

"You said that she claimed to be able to read palms," mused Nimino. "Not a clairvoyant then, not even a telepath as we understand the term, neither would have allowed themselves to fall into the position in which we found her. But she could have some barely suspected ability. Barely suspected by herself, I mean. How accurate was the reading?"

Dumarest looked up from the girl. "It was nothing," he

said flatly. "A jumble of nonsense. I could do as well myself."

"Perhaps she was not really trying," said the navigator shrewdly. "She is a girl who has learned the value of caution. And she is beautiful," he added. "Not often have I seen a woman of such loveliness. You have won a remarkable prize, my friend."

"Won?"

"But, of course, Earl. To the victor the spoils. Both of you must surely be aware of that." Nimino smiled and then grew serious. "Tell me exactly what happened just before she collapsed."

"We were talking," said Dumarest. "She dropped her hand to mine and touched my ring. That's when it happened."

"Your ring?"

Dumarest lifted his left hand. "This."

"I see." Nimino brooded as he examined the stone. "I ask no questions, my friend, but I will venture a statement. This ring has high emotional significance. To you and perhaps to the one who owned it before. Am I correct?"

"Yes," said Dumarest shortly.

"Then I think I understand what could have happened to Lallia. She is a sensitive of undeveloped and probably unsuspected power. There is an ability possessed by some by which they are able to tell the past of any object they may touch. It is almost as if they had a vision in which time unrolls before their awareness. I put it crudely, but you understand what I mean. And if the object has a strong emotional charge then the vision can become overpowering. I suggest that is what happened in the salon. She was excited, emotionally sensitive, and she touched your ring. It was as if she had received a sudden electrical discharge through the brain."

"And now?"

"Nothing, my friend." Nimino gripped Dumarest's shoulder. "She will sleep a little and wake as good as before. Her talent is untrained and undemanding and, as I said, probably she is not even aware of it other than the ability to read palms and tell fortunes. For time runs in both directions and such a one could have a limited awareness of events to come. Events appertaining to the object held, I mean. She is not a clairvoyant—as we both have reason to know."

Nimino dropped his hand as he moved towards the door of the cabin. "Let her wake and find you here, Earl. And, if you are afraid of demons, I know seven effective rites of exorcism. But I think the one she would appreciate most can only be performed by you."

Alone, Dumarest sat beside the bunk and closed his eyes as weariness assailed both mind and body. Demons, he thought, remembering Nimino's offer and suggestion. An old word for old troubles. The demons of hopelessness and hunger, of hate and the lust for revenge. The demons of ambition and greed, envy and desire. And the worst demon of all, perhaps, the cold, aching void of loneliness. A demon which could only be exorcised by love.

"Earl."

He opened his eyes. Lallia was awake, lying with her eyes on his face, the long length of her body relaxed, a thick coil of hair shadowing one side of her face. Her arms lifted as he stooped over her, white restraints pulling him down, holding him against the yielding softness of her body while her lips, soft and avid, found his own.

"Earl, my darling!" she whispered. "Earl!"

He could do nothing but sink into a warm and comforting sea.

They slept and woke to drink cups of basic and slept again in the warm cocoon of the cabin, lulled by the soft vibration of the Erhaft field as it sent the *Moray* arrowing to a distant world. Dumarest moved uneasily in his sleep, haunting dreams bringing him a montage of faces and places, of violence and blood, of hope and arid disappointment.

Finally he woke, refreshed, stretching his body and opening his eyes. Lallia stood at the side of the bunk, smiling, vapor rising from the cup in her hand.

"You're awake," she said. "Good. Now drink this."

It was basic but with an unusual flavor. He sipped appreciatively before emptying the container.

"I was a cook once," she said. "There's no need for basic to taste like wet mud. A few drops of flavoring can make all the difference."

He smiled. "And the flavor?"

"A few drops of the captain's precious oil. I raided the hold," she admitted. "That was after I'd fixed my passage with the navigator. He said that he could talk for the big boss. Can he?"

Dumarest nodded, Nimino handled details while the captain dreamed under the influence of his symbiote. "You didn't have to pay for passage," he commented. "That was a part of the deal."

"I know that, Earl." She sat beside him, serious, her eyes soft with emotion. "But that was only to the next planet of call. I want to stay with the ship, with you, so I arranged to ride all the way." She leaned towards him, the perfume of her body a clean scent of femininity. "We're married, Earl. A ship-marriage but married just the same." Her hand found his own, tightened. "You object?"

"No," said Dumarest. "I don't object."

"It will last as long as you stay on the *Moray*," she said. "As long as you want it to. A month, a year, ten years, a week, even; it doesn't matter. A marriage is good only as long as both partners want it to last. And I want it to last, Earl. I want it to last a long, long time."

She meant it, he decided, and found nothing objectionable about her or the idea. Lallia was all woman, a soft, yielding assembly of curves and tender flesh; but she was more than a sensuous animal designed to give pleasure. She was a creature who had learned to survive, a fit mate for a lonely traveler, a woman who could tend a wound and live on scraps as well as wear fine gowns and dine with nobility. Someone, perhaps, with whom to make a home.

He looked at her, reluctant to give up his dream of finding Earth, yet knowing that reality was preferable to a romantic quest. And yet need the dream be wholly discarded? Two could search as easily as one and it would be good not to have to travel alone.

"Earth?" She pondered the question, white teeth biting at her lower lip. "No, Earl, I've never heard of it. A planet, you say?"

"An old world, the surface scarred and torn by ancient wars, yet the interior holds a strange life. I was born there. I'm trying to get back."

She frowned. "But if you left the place you must know where it is. How to get back. Surely you have the coordinates?"

"No, Lallia, I haven't."

"But—"

"I was very young when I left," he interrupted. "I stowed away on a ship, frightened and desperate and knowing no better. The captain was an old man and treated me better than I deserved. He could have evicted me into space; instead he allowed me to join his crew under an oath of

secrecy. That was a long time ago now and he is safely dead.
I moved on, always heading deeper into the galaxy, moving
from world to world towards the Center. And Earth has
become less than a legend. The charts do not show it. No
one has ever heard of it. The very name has become mean-
ingless."

"It must be a very long way away," she said quietly.
"You must have traveled for a long time, Earl, my darling.
So long that your home planet has become lost among the
stars. And you want to find it again. But why? What is so
special about the place you ran away from that you must
find it again?"

Dumarest looked down at his hands and then back to
meet the level gaze of the woman. "A man must have some
reason for living," he said. "And Earth is my home."

"Home is where you make it, the place where you want
to be." Her hand fell to his arm, pressed. "Mine is with you,
Earl. It would be nice if you felt the same way about me."

He said, quietly, "Perhaps I do."

"Darling!"

He felt the soft touch of her hair as she pressed against
him, the smooth roundness of her cheek, the warmth of her
full, red lips. Her hand rose, caressing his hair, his face,
running over his shoulder and down his left arm, the fingers
pressing, moving on. He heard the sharp intake of her
breath as she touched his ring.

"Lallia?"

"I'm all right, Earl." She kissed him again then moved
away, eyes curious as she looked at the gem on his hand.
"When I touched that ring I felt the strangest sensation. It
was as if I heard someone crying, sobbing as if their heart
would break. Where did you get it, Earl?"

"It was a gift."

"From a woman?"

He smiled at the sharpness of her voice. "It came from a
woman," he admitted. "She is gone now."

"Dead?"

He nodded and she smiled, coming close to him again,
a female animal purring her satisfaction.

"I'm glad she's dead, Earl. I don't want to share you with
anyone. I think I'd kill any woman who tried to take you
from me. I know I'd kill anyone who hurt you. I love you,
my darling, always remember that."

Dumarest closed his arms around her as she again pressed

close. She was a creature of emotion, as honest as her temperament allowed, with the fiercely possessive nature of a primitive. But was that so very bad? She would be true to him according to her fashion and who could do more than that? And she was his wife, married to him according to Web trader custom, jealous of her rights.

"Earl?" Lallia stirred within the circle of his arms.

"What is it?"

"Nimino said that we're calling at Tyrann next. Have you ever been there?"

"No."

"That's good." She purred, moving even closer, snuggling against him. "Neither have I. We can explore it together."

Tyrann was a world of wind and scouring dust, of heat and eroded soil, a dying planet exploited for rare metals by men who looked with envious eyes at the beauty of the girl. A merchant, bolder than the rest, offered to buy her for the price of five High passages, doubling the offer when Dumarest refused.

Lallia was thoughtful as he escorted her back to the *Moray*. "You should have sold me, Earl. I could have sneaked out later and left the fool with nothing."

"A man like that is no fool," said Dumarest curtly. "And I am not a seller of women."

For the rest of their stay he kept Lallia within the confines of the ship while Sheyan negotiated a load of freight and Claude, happy in a tavern, stocked up on supplies.

From Tyrann they went to Dreen, where they delivered their freight and sold the fish skins. From Dreen to Ophan, where they left the oil and singing crystals, buying manufactured electronic components, capsules of medicine, and gaining three passengers: dour, silent men who refused to gamble despite Lallia's blandishments. The passengers and medicine were left behind on Frone as they plunged deeper into the Web. With them rode a dozen passengers bound for Joy.

"I will take," said Yalung slowly, "one card."

Dumarest dealt him the required card, relaxing a little as he threw in his own hand. The game was poker, the stakes running high, and they had been playing for twelve hours straight. He watched as Yalung bet, raised, was called, and raked in another pot. The dealer in precious stones had been a steady winner throughout the session.

One of the players rose, shaking his head.

"That's enough for me," he said. "Deal me out. I know when I'm outclased."

Dumarest scooped up the cards and shuffled, his eyes searching the faces of those who remained at the table. A miner, an engineer, a raddled woman who smelled of acrid spice, a seller of chemical dreams, and Yalung, who sat to his right. In the light their faces were taut masks of inner concentration.

"The pot is ten," said Dumarest and, as chips were thrust forward, began to deal. "Openers are a pair of jesters or better."

The miner passed, the engineer also, the woman opened for ten. The seller of dreams stayed and Yalung raised the bet to twenty. Dumarest took a quick look at his cards. A lord, a lady, two eights and a three.

"Dealer stays."

The miner dropped out and the engineer stayed, which meant that he had either passed on an opening hand or hoped to improve. The woman stayed as did the seller of dreams.

"Discards."

Dumarest watched the players as he poised the deck, not their faces, they were schooled to display only desired emotion, but their hands which told more than their owners guessed. The engineer flipped his cards, moving one from one end of the fand to the others. Adding it to others of the same value? Arranging a sequence?

"I'll take three."

He held a pair then, probably of low value because he hadn't opened. Dumarest dealt and turned to the woman.

"Two," she said.

She had opened and must have at least a pair of jesters. A two-card draw meant that she might have three of a kind or was holding onto an odd card, hoping to make two pairs or more, or, more likely, in order to bluff. She hadn't raised Yalung's increase—unlikely if her hand had been strong.

Beside her sat the seller of dreams. Envir had a thin, intent face, which told nothing, and hands which told little more. He moved a pair of cards, hesitated, then threw out his discards.

"I'll take two," he said.

Like the woman he could have either a pair or three of

a kind. He could also be hoping to complete a flush or a straight, in which case he was fighting high odds.

"One," said Yalung.

He had not fiddled with his cards, his hands, like his face, unrevealing. He could have four to a flush or a straight, two pairs, three of a kind and an odd card, or even four of a kind.

Dumarest threw out his own discards. "Dealer takes three."

He let them lie, watching the hands of the others, the tiny, betraying tensions of their knuckles as they saw what they had drawn.

"Twenty," said the woman. It was a safe, normal opening bet. Envir raised it.

"Make that fifty."

Yalung pushed chips into the pot. "I'll raise that fifty more."

Dumarest looked at his cards. He had drawn another eight and a pair of ladies. A full house.

"Dealer raises that by fifty."

The engineer hesitated, scowling, then threw in his hand. The woman stayed. Envir cleared his throat.

"Well, now, this promises to be fun. I'll just meet that last raise—and lift it another two hundred."

"That's two hundred and fifty to stay," mused Yalung. "I'll raise by another hundred."

Dumarest looked at the pot. It held over a thousand. If he raised it would give him a chance to raise again later—but both Envir and Yalung had seemed confident. The woman, he guessed, would drop out. Envir might stay, in which case the pot would go to the one with the best hand.

"Dealer stays," said Dumarest.

He thought he saw a shadow of disappointment cross Yalung's face, then turned his attention to the others. The woman, as he had guessed, threw in her cards, displaying the pair of jesters on which she had opened. Envir hesitated then made his decision.

"I'll raise a hundred."

"One hundred?" Yalung leaned forward, counting the chips in the pot. "There is just over seventeen hundred there," he mused. "According to the rules I am allowed to raise to the full extent of the pot. So I will do that. I meet your raise, my friend, and add another fifteen hundred." He smiled at Dumarest. "It will now cost the dealer sixteen hundred to stay. An interesting situation, is it not?"

"No," said Dumarest flatly. "I cannot stay. I haven't the money."

"But surely you have items of worth?" Yalung looked at Dumarest's hand. "That ring, for example. Shall we say a thousand?"

It was a tempting proposition. Envir had drawn two cards and could be pushing his luck with a straight or flush, both of which he could beat. Yalung could be bluffing, using his money to buy the pot, also maybe holding a flush or straight. But, against that, Dumarest could only gain to one for his money if Envir dropped out and, if he raised, he would be unable to stay.

"Dealer drops out," said Dumarest, and threw in his cards.

He heard the quick intake of breath from those who stood around the table, Lallia among the watchers, Lin at her side.

Envir sucked in his cheeks and slowly counted his chips. "Damn it," he said. "Damn all the luck. Well, to hell with it. I think you're bluffing." He pushed forward a pile of chips. "I'll see you!"

Yalung slowly put three tens on the table. "Is that enough?"

"Like hell it is!" The seller of dreams glowed his excitement. "I've got a flush. That means I win."

"Not quite." Yalung put down the rest of his cards. An ace and another ten. "Four tens. The pot is mine, I think?"

Envir cursed in his disappointment.

VII

JOY WAS at carnival.

Streamers of colored smoke hung in the air, luminous in the dying light, and from all sides rose the sound of music and gaiety. Tents, booths, collapsible shops, the open rings of combat and the closed enclaves of sensory titivation, jugglers, tumblers, contortionists, men who promised eternal happiness, and harpies who roved, hard-eyed and falsely charming, offering pleasure to those who had come to join in the fun.

"We could do well here," said Lallia as she stood beside Dumarest at the head of the ramp. "When it gets really dark I could get to work. Drunken fools won't object to a woman's caress and they'll be too bemused to guard their pockets. With you to take care of any trouble we could clean up."

"No," said Dumarest.

"Why not?" Her tone was mocking. "Morals, lover?"

"Sense. The risk is too great for the reward."

"We need money," she insisted. "Your share is hardly enough to buy me some new clothes. Can you think of a better way to get it, Earl?"

He ignored the question, looking instead at the ships littering the field. Mostly they were old, battered, traders like the *Moray*, but a few were new and one was big. A vessel strange to the Web and one which could be heading Outside. The woman at his side he walked towards it, climbing the ramp to the open port. Shadows moved within the dim interior and a man, neat in his uniform, eyes and face hard, stepped before him.

"You want something?"

"A berth if it's going."

"You from the *Moray*?"

"Yes," said Dumarest.

"Then forget it," said the man. "There's no berth going especially to anyone from that hulk." He glanced at Lallia. "Your woman?"

"His wife," said Lallia. "What have you got against the *Moray*?"

"Personally, nothing," admitted the man. "But her reputation stinks. If you'll take my advice you'll forget to mention her. Say you're from the *Argos* or the *Deltara*—both of those left just before the carnival."

"I'll remember that," said Dumarest. "If you haven't got a berth then how about traveling Low?"

"That might be possible." The man hesitated. "Look, I can't give you a definite answer until the captain tells me what space we'll have available. You'd better come back later—we're not due out for a couple of days yet but as far as I know if you can pay you'll get passage. Fair enough?"

"Thanks," said Dumarest. "I'll be seeing you."

He was thoughtful as he walked towards the edge of the field. The other ships would be similar, with only a single man in charge or locked while their crews went about their business or pleasure. Lallia touched his arm.

"Did you mean that, Earl? About leaving, I mean?"

"Yes."

"And me?"

She was worried, he could tell it by the way she clung to his arm, the expression in her eyes. "You'll come with me," he promised. "The Web is no place for a woman to be stranded."

Her smile was his reward. "Thank you, lover. Now let's go and get ourselves some fun."

They passed from the field into a welter of noise, confusion, and frantic activity punctuated by shouts, shrieks, and bellowing laughter. A procession weaved down the street, monstrous heads bobbing in fabricated distortion, voices echoing from the diminutive bodies. A troupe of zingart dancers spun and stamped, froth bubbling their lips, naked bodies scarred with symbolic designs. Their hair was fuzzed into gigantic balls, nose and ears pierced with skewers, bells around wrists, neck, and ankles. Two dwarfs scuttled beside them, collecting boxes rattling as they thrust them before the watchers.

The zingart dancers were followed by a dozen flagellants, chanting as they each lashed the other with spiked whips. The flagellants passed and a host of women rotated bellies and breasts as they clustered around a tall, bearded anchorite. After them came a cluster of masked and decorated figures, some with whips hanging from their wrists, others with tufts of spiked fur.

Something exploded high above and the darkening sky shone brilliant with a gush of luminous stars.

Dumarest followed Lallia as she pushed her way through the crowd. The lustrous mane of her hair reflected the colorful embers above, their dying light illuminating her long legs as they flashed beneath the hem of her iridescent dress. A masked reveler, one of a group of the local nobility, caught her arm as she passed.

"Come, my sweeting," he purred. "Such tender flesh should not pass uncaressed." He dropped both hands to her shoulders, forcing the material from her rounded breasts, his head dipping as he pressed his lips against her body.

Dumarest paused, watching, his muscles tense. Lallia did not seem to object to the rough treatment. She laughed and pressed herself closer to the gaudy finery the man wore. And then suddenly he cried out and thrust her away.

"Bitch! You she-devil! I'll teach you to hurt your betters!"

His hand bent, caught the whip dangling from his wrist, raised it high to slash across her face. He cried out again as Dumarest caught the raised hand, his fingers closing hard against yielding bone.

"You are excited, my lord," said Dumarest coldly. "I think it best that you take a little rest."

Abruptly he pushed, catching the man off-balance, thrusting him to sprawl in the road among the feet of dancing monstrosities. He rolled, trying to avoid the kicks of enlarged feet, soiling his finery with dirt and liquid filth.

Dumarest caught Lallia by the arm and urged her from the scene of the incident.

Laughing she held up a purse. "You see, lover, how easy it is? That fool was too intent on what he wanted to miss this. When I had it I hit him where it hurts. Shall we do it again?"

"No."

"But, lover, we need the stake. Why miss the chance?"

"He wasn't alone," said Dumarest. "And you are rather unmistakable. When he misses his money he will come looking and his friends with him. I don't think they will be very gentle if they find you."

Lallia shrugged. "So?"

"So we find you something else to wear." Dumarest looked at the purse in her hand. "And you can pay for it.

The merchant was an old man with a stoop so pronounced that it gave him the appearance of a tall, thin bird of prey; an impression heightened by his hooked nose and balding head. He fingered Lallia's dress and sucked in his cheeks.

"It is good," he admitted. "Fine and unusual material, but the customers for such are few. I am far from the field and must depend on local trade. It could lie for months and then, perhaps, I would have to sell it at a fraction of its worth."

"That's all I'm asking," said Lallia. She had taken charge of the transaction as soon as she had entered the shop. "One of your gowns, a coat, some other things. You should make a fat profit."

"My dear, you are a shrewd woman but you know little of local conditions. At carnival everyone goes mad, but normally a woman would be stoned for wearing a thing like this. However . . ."

Dumarest turned away as the haggling progressed. Outside, in the narrow street beyond the shop, the throb and hum of carnival was very faint. The sky had darkened rapidly and a few stars shone in competition with the uprushing pyrotechnics. Two men wearing the unmistakable uniform of guards entered the street and loped past the shop. They seemed to be looking for someone and Dumarest could guess who it was."

"Hurry," he said turning to where the pair stood over a heap of clothing. "Take a gown, Lallia, something to cover your legs. And something else to cover your hair. Fancy dress will do."

The merchant looked up, his eyes shrewd. "And the dress she is wearing?"

"I'll continue to wear it," said Lallia firmly. She probed into the stolen purse for coins. "How much do I owe?"

"For the carnival costume, fifteen coryms." The man held out his hand as Lallia frowned at the coins. "Those seven-sided pieces are of five coryms each. Three will settle the bill." He nodded as she dropped the coins into his palm. "You may change at the rear, my dear. There will be no extra charge."

She returned wearing a long robe which touched the ground, sleeves falling past the tips of her fingers and a high headdress which completely covered her hair and gave an oval look to her face. The merchant handed her a mask.

"With this on your face, my dear, no one will recognize you."

"Should I worry if they do?" Lallia caught his hand and stared into the palm. "I read hands," she said quietly. "For five coryms I will read yours."

The merchant tugged at his hand. "Please, I have no time for such nonsense."

"Nonsense?" Lallia shook her head. "You be the judge. In your hand I see daughters of whom you are ashamed and sons who have caused you much grief, a third—" She frowned. "The third is the source of much heartbreak."

"Arnobalm," the merchant said quietly. "He has been ill since his youth. A virus disease for which there is no known cure. At least it is not known in the Web. Unless it is checked he will die within a season."

"But you have hope?" Lallia twisted the aged palm. "I read that you have much hope."

"It is all that is left. The expense is high but what is money when compared to life? And his faith is strong. Perhaps, on Shrine, he will be above to recover from the thing which saps at his life." The merchant pulled free his hand. "You have seen the ship, perhaps? With it rides the prayers and hopes of a hundred parents, a thousand relatives." He saw their expressions. "You do not know of Shrine?"

Dumarest shook his head.

"But you are of space, that I can tell by your uniform. Is it possible that the miracle planet is a stranger to you?"

"I come from Outside," said Dumarest. "The woman also. Traders."

"And traders are not interested in miracles, only in profits." The merchant sighed. "I understand. You are long on Joy?"

"A few hours."

"And you will leave with the carnival," said the merchant. "You space traders! Always on the move, never stopping, never putting down roots. But you have chosen a good time. There is much to see on Joy when the carnival is here. Exhibitions, a zoo, places of instruction." A shadow crossed his face. "And other things . . . but I will not spoil your pleasure." He bowed and ushered them towards the door.

Outside Lallia drew a deep breath. "He robbed us," she said. "You know that, I suppose. Why didn't you let me try to get some of it back?"

"By telling him lies?"

"What I read in his palm was true."

"And something he already knew." Dumarest took her arm. "Now empty that purse and get rid of it somewhere. And don't worry about the old man having robbed you. You bought more than a costume, you paid for his silence, he could have called the guards."

"And lost his profit." Lallia shrugged. "All right, Earl, you're the boss. Now for God's sake, let's get a drink."

They found a tavern, bright with tinsel, glowing with luminous paint and throbbing with interior noise and laughter. Claude came lurching through the door as they approached. The engineer's face was blotched, his eyes glazed, the front of his uniform stained with wine. He swayed and recovered his balance with a visible effort. Wine gurgled from the bottle he held in his hand, drenching his chin and adding to the wetness on his chest.

"Earl!" He gestured with the bottle. "My old friend! Have a drink."

Dumarest took the bottle and held it to his closed lips. "Thanks."

"And you?" The engineer almost fell again as he leaned to stare at Lallia. "Who are you?"

She raised her mask and reached for the bottle. "Who

do you think, you drunken idiot? Do you imagine I'd let Earl loose with another woman?"

"Not you!" He roared with laughter as she drank and returned the bottle. Waving it he turned and yelled at the tavern. "Make way for the most beautiful woman in space! A real woman! And you know what? She belongs to the *Moray!*"

Lin came through the door as the engineer staggered away. The steward was anxious as he stared after his mentor.

"He's gone crazy, Earl. You'd think he hadn't touched a drink for years the way he's going on. What can I do?"

"Nothing," said Dumarest. "Forget him."

Lin was firm. "I can't do that, Earl. He's my friend."

"And a man should be loyal to his friends," agreed Dumarest. "But he should pick his friends. Claude's a drunk and there's nothing you can do about it. At any moment he could go kill-crazy and you could be on the receiving end. A man like that is dangerous. Why don't you forget him and enjoy yourself?"

"I couldn't," said the steward simply. "Not if I know he needs me. Tell me what to do, Earl?"

"Follow him. Pick him up if he falls down. Try to see that he doesn't get robbed and, when he passes out, get help to carry him back to the ship."

A friend, thought Dumarest as Lin moved away. Someone the engineer didn't deserve and didn't appreciate. And Claude? A father image to the boy, a surrogate parent who taught and held a tarnished glory. Only Lin wouldn't believe that it was tarnished. He would put his trust in his hero and maybe it would break his heart when realization finally came.

"A nice boy." Lallia's voice was low. "It would be wonderful to have a son like that, Earl."

"Yes," said Dumarest.

"Perhaps, one day, we shall." Her hand tightened on his arm. "When we settle down, Earl. When we find a place we can call home." Her grip tightened even more. "And soon, Earl. Soon."

Soon, before it was too late—if it was not too late already.

Inside the tavern was filled with men and laughing girls; the men, mostly spacers, somber in their uniforms against the carnival dress worn by residents and visitors. Girls swung between the crowded benches carrying great jugs of wine and beer, trays of cakes and pastries, fried meats wrapped in crisp batter, fish which had been gilded in gold and silver and glowing red. Dumarest bought a bottle of wine, a handful of cakes, and two of the fish, carrying them to a table surrounded by a medley of uniforms.

"Those you can keep," said Lallia, pushing aside the fish. "I've had enough seafood to last the rest of my life." She bit into one of the cakes as Dumarest poured the wine, swallowing as she picked up the glass. "Here's health!"

They drank. The wine was dark, full-bodied, easy to throat and stomach. Dumarest savored it as he picked up one of the fish. The flesh was white and delicately sweet. Around them talk hummed like a swarm of bees.

"—told him the load would go bad without . . . fifteen, I said, and not one less . . . the *Giesha* didn't show at rendezvous so we took . . . tried to sell us some stuff which any fool would have known . . . that drunken idiot from the *Moray?*"

Dumarest looked up as he sipped his wine, his attention caught by the name of the trader. A broad back was talking to a high forehead.

"I saw him," said the high forehead. "Rolling all over the place. No man can drink like that and remain sharp. He's only got to let the generators get point oh, oh five out of phase and you know what happens then."

"Curtains," said the broad back. "Disorientation and, in the Web, that's bad."

"That's final!" The high forehead was emphatic. "Say, did you hear about the *Quand?* I met a man on . . ."

Lallia smiled at Dumarest as he turned, lowering his glass. "We don't have to worry, Earl. We won't be on the *Moray* when Claude finally sends her to destruction."

"No," he said, thinking of Lin, the burning desire of the boy to learn, to emulate his friend. Suddenly the wine tasted sour. "Let's go and look at the town."

The main street led to an area thronged with sideshows. A man called as they passed. "This way, lord and lady, sense the thrills of the condemned. Full sensory tapes of those who have met death by burning, hanging, poisoning, and dismemberment. Not to be bettered in the entire Web!"

Another, "Two more wanted for the love-raffle! Come and share in erotic delights!"

Another, "Trained symbiotes from Phadar! Exotic thrills for an ounce of blood!

A painted crone tittered as they passed her booth gaudy

with mystic signs. "Read your future, dearie? Find out if the fine young man means what he says."

"He means it, mother," said Lallia hanging to Dumarest's arm. "I'll see to that."

A fire-eater blew long streamers of brilliance. A girl writhed to the monotonous pounding of a drum. A squat, amorphous creature snarled and rattled heavy chains. From before a billowing tent a woman called in a voice of trained allurement:

"You there, master! Care to fight for your lady? Ten-inch blades and first blood the winner. A prize for all contestants and, if you win, fifty coryms and the choice of five willing wantons."

Lallia was curt. "Go to hell, you painted bitch!"

The woman, a blonde, curvaceous of body, smiled with a lifting of her full, red lips. "What's the matter, honey? Can't stand the competition? Or are you afraid good-looking will get himself hurt?"

"Make it five hundred and he'll fight to the death!"

The woman blinked. "Say, do you mean that? If you do a match can be arranged. How about coming up here to discuss the deal?"

"Forget it," snapped Dumarest.

"Why, Earl?" Lallia looked up into his face as he pulled her away from the tent. "I've seen you fight, remember? The pugs they've got in there wouldn't stand a chance against your speed. And we could use five hundred coryms."

"I'll fight if I have to," he said curtly. "But I don't do it for fun. And it wouldn't be a fair combat. The opponent would be helped all along the line. Lights fixed to dazzle, attention-catchers, even a gimmicked blade. I've even known them to use a gas-spray to slow a man down."

"You've worked in the circuits," she said slowly. "You didn't tell me that, Earl."

"There's a lot I didn't tell you."

"But you could win," she insisted. "You know that."

He halted and looked into her eyes. "Listen, girl, there's no such thing as a certainty. Every time a man fights he gambles his life. So far I've won but that doesn't mean that I can't lose. It could be this time, in that tent, is that what you want?"

"You know it isn't, Earl."

"Then forget it." Gently he lifted his hands and dropped

them on her shoulders, squeezing before turning away.
"Let's look at the rest of the carnival."

A crowd thronged around a table on which a man manipulated cards. Dumarest won thirty coryms by finding the
jester, spent half a corym on a mass of sticky sweetmeat for
Lallia and paused before a booth. Young men were practic-
ing their skill by throwing knives at a target. The leather-
lunged operator saw the couple and called an invitation.

"A corym for six blades, my lord. A prize for getting
them all in the center."

Dumarest paid his coin and hefted the knives. They were
badly balanced, crudely fashioned, and showed marks of
wear. But they had a point and that was enough. His arm
rose, the hand moving forward, the knife a blur as it left
his fingers. The thud as it hit the target was repeated five
more times.

"You win, my lord!" The operator looked anxious. "A set
of six entitles you to anything on display."

Lallia chose a doll, a pretty thing with long, silken hair
and clothes of finely spun fabric.

"You wish to play again, my lord?" The operator smiled
his relief as Dumarest shook his head. "It can be done," he
bawled as the pair moved away. "You have seen it! Roll up
and test your skill!"

"So you can throw knives, Earl," said Lallia as they
walked past the glittering booths. "What else don't I know
about you? Never mind," she said, not waiting for an answer.
"I'll find out. I've a lifetime to do it in. Right, lover?"

He looked at her, tall, beautiful, the doll cradled in her
arms, and felt a sudden wave of tenderness. It would be
good to find somewhere to settle down, to build a home,
and to find immortality in children. Good enough, perhaps,
to eliminate his need to search for a forgotten world.

"Look!" Lallia pointed to where an arched opening stood
before them. "Freaks and interstellar zoo," she read. "Can
we go in, Earl?"

A man stepped forward as they passed into the area beyond the arch. He was old with a sunken face and eyes
which held a burning intensity.

"My lord and lady," he said. "I beg of your charity. For
the love of all you hold sacred help the pilgrims to Shrine."

Lallia looked around. "Pilgrims?"

"Those within, my lady." The man gestured towards the

opening of a tent. "The animals are beyond, but the others need no cage."

"The freaks?" Lallia frowned. "I thought you said they were pilgrims."

"They are both, my lady. The journey is long and costly so they display their infirmities in order to raise funds. It is not a pleasant thing to do but what is pride against necessity?"

The interior of the tent was dim with a pale green lighting which threw no shadows and yet was gentle to the eyes. A score or more of figures sat or sprawled against the walls on heaped piles of rags. Many appeared to be asleep. All were grotesquely deformed.

"Medical science cannot aid them." The man had accompanied Lallia and Dumarest into the tent. "They are transplant immune, or they are so distorted that nothing can be done. There are others who suffer less visible infirmity, those with strange diseases and stranger internal growths, but these are not on display."

"And all are bound for Shrine?" asked Dumarest.

"That is so, my lord. There, if their faith is strong, they will be cured. The weak shall rise and walk, the crippled stand straight and tall, the deformed be relieved of their afflictions." He held out his collecting bowl. "Of your charity, my lord. I beg it in their name." He stared as Dumarest poured coins into the bowl. "My lord! Our thanks for your generosity. May good fortune attend you."

Outside Lallia said, "You're crazy, Earl. That or soft. Why did you give him so much?"

"You've been stranded," said Dumarest quietly. "You know what it's like. But you had your health and strength. Can you imagine what it must be like for those poor devils?"

"You're right, Earl, I'm sorry." She bit her lip and then, brightening, said, "Well, it's done and good luck to them. Let's go and look at the animals."

They were a poor collection, beasts from a dozen worlds, furred, clawed, tailed, and armored; most were offshoots of the animals men had taken with them, a few native to local planets. A scaled thing chittered and threshed its wings. A legged snake crawled, eyes like jewels, jaws agape to show a darting tongue. A thing of tendrils and wirelike hair swung in a tight ball from the top of its cage. The air was thick with a dozen odors.

A straggle of revelers hung around the cages, a small

group standing before one containing a furred, manlike creature, laughing as they tormented it with their whips and the thrusts of long canes. Dumarest looked towards them, past them, narrowing his eyes as he caught a flash of yellow. Yalung? The figure was the same but he had only caught a glimpse—and yellow and black were common colors during a festival.

Lallia shrugged when he mentioned it. "The dealer? No, I didn't see him, but if he's here what of it? I guess he has to relax sometime, like the rest of us."

She wandered off, intent on the animals, leaving Dumarest behind. He stood, barely interested in the exhibition, waiting until the girl had slaked her curiosity. He watched as she moved towards the cage holding the tormented beast. A man laughed as she protested, and he deliberately thrust again with his cane. The beast stirred, smashing at the stick and tearing it from the man's grasp. Incensed he struck at it with his whip.

"Don't!" Lallia caught at his arm.

"Get away from me, you bitch!"

He pushed, sending the woman sprawling, lifting his whip to strike again. A tuft of fur and blood sprang from the point of impact. The beast roared and flung itself against the bars. Abruptly the entire front of the cage swung open with a grate of yielding metal.

"Lallia!" Dumarest was running as the animal sprang from the cage, one swipe of its paw sending its tormentor hurtling to one side with a crushed skull. "Lallia!"

She moved, crouching on the ground, eyes terrified as she looked at the beast advancing towards her. It was a mutated sport, five feet tall with the body of a gorilla and the fangs, teeth, and muzzle of a bear. As she rose it snarled and jumped towards her.

Dumarest met it in midair.

It was like hitting a wall, a compact mass of bone and sinew three times the weight of a man. He felt himself fall, the sour reek of the thing's breath harsh in his nostrils, and rolled desperately to avoid the raking claws. They rose together, the beast lightning fast, and Dumarest knew that to run would be suicide. He sprang forward before the creature could wholly regain its balance, ramming the top of his skull under the lower jaw, wedging his boots between the hind legs and locking his arms around the furred barrel of the chest.

He strained, muscles cracking as he tried to break the animal's spine. His body was an arched bow, head and feet pressing hard into throat and groin. The teeth couldn't hurt him, the claws on the hind legs couldn't reach him but he could do nothing about the vicious claws on the forepaws. He felt them rip at his shoulders and back, tearing the plastic of his uniform and ripping into the flesh beneath.

Again he heaved, the breath choking in his lungs, face turned to avoid the smothering mat of fur. It was as if he pulled against a mountain. He tensed, straightening so as to press the creature's head back so that it looked at the sky. It snarled and tore at his sides as he strained against the rigid back, knowing that his only chance was to break neck or spine.

He felt something yield and the beast whimpered, a small sound deep in its chest. Gritting his teeth, Dumarest summoned the last of his strength.

"Yalung!" He heard Lallia's shout above the roar of blood in his ears. "Good God's sake, hurry!"

The beast whimpered again, yielding even more and then, suddenly, convulsed with an explosion of energy which sent Dumarest staggering to one side, to fall and rise fighting for breath, shaking his head to clear the mist from his eyes.

He saw the animal lying dead, Yalung standing over it with a rod of iron in his hands, the end of the improvised spear thick with blood.

"Earl!" Lallia ran towards him, eyes enormous in the pallor of her face. "My God, Earl, your back!"

He straightened, feeling the burn of multiple lacerations, and looking down saw that his sides and legs were drenched with blood. More blood made a puddle on the ground. The claws of the beast had ripped wide and deep.

And, suddenly, there was pain.

VIII

LALLIA SAID, "I'm sorry, Earl. I had no choice. There was nothing else to do but get you back to the *Moray*."

Dumarest looked at her from where he lay on the bunk. She was wearing the iridescent dress and the thick coils of her midnight hair hung loose about her shoulders. The light gleamed from the naked flesh of her arms, the long curves of her thighs.

"You had a choice," he said quietly. "You could have taken me to a local doctor."

"Yes," she admitted. "I could but I didn't think of it. You were in a hell of a mess, passing out with weakness and pain, and Yalung seemed to know just what to do. He washed you down and shot you full of dope and antibiotics. At first I thought of moving you before it was too late but Sheyan left early. The rest you know."

A time of pain interspersed with gulps of basic, the sting of antiseptics, the discomfort of changed dressings. Of drug-induced sleep and the sparing magic of slowtime. Dumarest sat upright and looked at his naked body, seeing the thin lines of scar tissue on his sides. There would be more on his back and shoulders: newly healed wounds which would eventually harden.

"A local doctor could have got me fit within two days," he said. "Using slowtime and intravenous feeding. But it would have cost money. Did you think of that?"

Lallia met his eyes. "At first, no, but I did later. All right, Earl, so I begrudged the cost. It would have taken all we had and I didn't fancy us being stranded on Joy. And what's the difference? So we didn't quit the *Moray*, but there will be another chance later."

Dumarest rose and looked down at the woman. He saw the pallor of fatigue, the lines of weariness marring her beauty. She could have left him. She could have let him die. Instead she had sat beside him in constant attendance.

"You're tired," he said. "Lie down and get some rest."

"I'm all right, Earl."

"Do it." He stooped and lifted her from the chair. "I don't want you losing your beauty."

"As long as you want me, Earl." She clung to him. "Any way you want," she whispered. "But just keep wanting."

He smiled and pressed her to the bunk. Turning he opened the lockers. His uniform had been ruined and he had the choice of wearing the protective clothing or those he had worn before joining the ship. He chose his own, slipping into the gray plastic, the material comforting in its protection. Had he worn it on Joy the claws of the beast would never have penetrated the wire mesh buried in the material. The knife fell as he adjusted the tunic and he thrust it into his boot.

LALLIA

"That's better." Lallia looked at him as he stood beside the bunk. "You never did look quite at home in that handler's uniform."

"Go to sleep," he said, closing the lockers. Turning off the light he stepped from the cabin.

Yalung looked up from the table as Dumarest entered the salon, watching as he drew a cup of basic, refilling it twice more before setting it down.

"You were hungry," said the dealer. "A healthy sign. You are fully recovered?"

"Yes." Dumarest looked at the yellow face, the enimgatic eyes. "I must thank you for coming to my aid with that spear. And again for looking after me."

"The woman did that." A scatter of gems lay on the surface of the table, tiny lights winking from their facets. "She tended you as if you were her child. My own part was small. If I could offer advice I would suggest that you conserve your strength. The wounds were stubborn to heal. The claws of the beast must have carried a mutated infection. Once I despaired for your life." His hand touched the gems. "I gathered from the woman that you intended to leave us at Joy."

"I'd thought of it."

"A man needs money in the Web. It may help if I bought your ring. A thousand as offered."

Dumarest shook his head.

"Of course," mused Yalung, "if it has an interesting history I could offer more. The value of such things is enhanced by an attendant story. If you would care to tell me of its origins, how you obtained it, details like that I could, perhaps, offer fifteen hundred."

"The ring is not for sale," said Dumarest shortly. "Again I give you my thanks for your attentions."

Yalung bowed. "Perhaps you will accommodate me in a hand of cards?"

"Later," said Dumarest, and left the salon.

Outside, in the passage, he hesitated, then made his way towards Nimino's cabin. The navigator smiled as he entered.

"Earl, my friend, you are fit and well. Truly my appeals have been answered. Laugh if you wish but the beliefs of millions cannot be ignored. I have burned sweet scents to Shume, the goddess of healing, on your behalf and she has answered my pleas."

"This?" Dumarest glanced to where a metal bowl held a

83

smoldering substance and painted symbols lay in careful arrangement around a globe of crystal in which drifted colored motes.

Nimino shook his head, abruptly solemn. "No, my friend, this is not for you. For many hours now I have been troubled by a sense of impending doom. It is as if, somewhere, a storm was pending but I do not know where or when it will break. I am disturbed and ill at ease. You sense nothing?"

"No," said Dumarest.

"Nor Lallia?"

"She is asleep."

"Then I am alone." Nimino shivered, a sudden convulsion of his nerves. "I hope it is nothing, but once, when I felt like this, a city was lost in an unexpected eruption. The Kharma Ball warned that I should leave."

Dumarest knelt and looked at the crystal ball, his hands resting on the floor to either side. The colored motes were, he guessed, fragments of organic life drifting in a supporting medium. Their purpose he couldn't imagine but he assumed they would be affected by vibration or sonic impulses.

Vibration?

He tensed, concentrating on the tips of his fingers. Rising he placed them against the metal bulkhead. The faint quiver of the Erhaft field was easily felt.

"Nimino," he said quietly. "Check the field." He waited until the navigator had placed his slender fingers on the metal and then said, "Can you feel it?"

"Yes, Earl." Nimino's eyes grew wide, pools of glistening brilliance in the darkness of his face. "So this is what I sensed!"

The quivering pulse of the heart of the ship. The tiny vibration which was the only discernible sign of its correct working.

A vibration which was not as it should be.

Dumarest heard Lin's voice as they ran towards the engine room.

"Claude! I tell you the dials are showing red! You've got to do something!"

"Shut your mouth!" The engineer's voice was a raging bellow. "Are you trying to tell me my job? You, a snotty-nosed kid still wet behind the ears?"

"But, Claude!" The steward was desperate. "The manual

says that when the panel looks like that the generators are getting out of phase. For God's sake, put down that bottle and do something. Do you want to wreck the ship?"

Dumarest heard a shout, the crash of something shattering, the fall of something heavy. Claude glared from behind his console as he and the navigator burst into the room.

"Get out!" he said. "The pair of you. I don't want anyone in my engine room."

Quietly Nimino said, "Earl, he's drunk. Look at his eyes."

Claude was more than drunk. The devil inside had broken loose in a gust of savage violence. Dumarest looked at the limp body lying on the floor. Lin lay in a puddle of liquid, the smashed remnants of a bottle lying beside his head. A trickle of blood ran from beneath his hair. It ceased as he watched. The steward would never now realize his ambition. He would never join the big ships and see the worlds outside the Web. His friend, his father-surrogate, had seen to that.

Dumarest took three steps towards where the engineer stood by his console.

"You killed him," he said coldly. "You killed the boy."

"Stay away from me!" Metal shone as Claude lifted his hand. A wrench was gripped in the big fingers. "Come any closer and I'll crack your skull."

"Like you did to Lin?" Dumarest stooped, anger a cold fire in his brain, his fingers reaching for the knife in his boot.

Nimino caught his arm. "No, Earl. He's our engineer. We need him."

"We don't need him," said Dumarest. "He's a drunken, useless fool. He must have seen that the generators were getting out of phase but couldn't do anything about it. So he started to drink in order to forget. He kept on drinking. Now he's crazy."

"You—"

The wrench swept up and forward, light glinting on the spinning metal as it left the big hand, the heavy thing aimed directly at Dumarest's head. He ducked, straightening as the engineer sprang towards him, tasting blood as a big fist slammed into his mouth. The blow rocked him backwards and, before he could recover, Claude had gripped him by the throat.

"Crazy, am I? A drunken, stupid fool. Well, handler, this is where it ends. I'm going to kill you."

His hands tightened, constricting clamps of flesh and

bone. Above the twin ridges of his arms Dumarest could see his face, the broad, mottled surface contorted with insane rage. That rage gave the engineer immense strength. He picked up Dumarest and slammed him back against the edge of the console, the metal rim digging cruelly into his spine, sending waves of agony from the barely healed wounds.

"Claude!" Nimino sprang forward, tugging at the engineer's arms. "Don't! Let him go, he—"

A vicious jerk of an elbow sent the navigator staggering to one side. Dumarest lifted both his hands and thrust them between the rigid forearms. He pressed, forcing his own arms between those of the engineer, thumbs reaching for the eyes. Claude snarled and jerked back his head.

Dumarest snatched back his hands and lifted them to the fingers clamped around his throat. He couldn't breathe and lacked strength, but his brain worked with icy calm. Trapped as he was against the edge of the console he could neither reach his knife or use his feet or knees. Maniacal rage had turned the engineer's arms into rods of steel and it was impossible to reach his eyes. But he could reach the fingers.

He gripped each of the smallest and pulled. It was like pulling at a steel restraint. Darkness began to edge his vision and a raw agony grew within his lungs. He pulled again, ignoring the pain of his back and sides as the new scar tissue yielded beneath the strain. The little fingers lifted and he wrapped his hands around them jerking with the last of his strength.

Bone snapped. Claude cried out, an animal sound of hurt and pain, snatching free his hands and stepping backwards. Nimino rose like a shadow behind him, the wrench a flashing arc in his hand. The sound of its impact was that of a squashing melon.

"Earl, are you all right?"

Dumarest nodded, massaging his throat. Another ten seconds and he would have used feet and hands to smash down the engineer but Nimino hadn't given him the time. Now he stood, looking at the wrench, the slumped figure lying in a pool of blood.

"He's dead," he said dully. "I killed him. Earl, I killed him!"

"He was insane. You had no choice."

"There is always a choice." The wrench fell from the navigator's hand. "I have taken a life," he said. "That means I have to return to the beginning and commence again the long and painful climb towards the Ultimate. It would have been better for me had I allowed you to use your knife."

"He would still have been dead," said Dumarest. He was impatient with the navigator's brooding introspection, his concern with a problematical afterlife. "The only difference is that I would have intended to kill him. You did not. He must have had a thin skull."

"Fate," said Nimino thoughtfully. "Who can fight against it? It was my destiny to kill a man." He looked at the console, at the mass of signal lights brightly red. "As it is our destiny to die. Claude has, perhaps, cheated us. He had an easy ending."

Dumarest was curt. "Explain."

"The generators are out of phase, my friend. The error is increasing. When it reaches a certain point the forces we have utilized to move us at supralight speeds will tear us apart."

"Couldn't we land before that happens?" asked Dumarest. "Turn off the generators to conserve their effective life?"

"Can we fight against our destiny?"

"We can fight." Dumarest looked down at his hands, they were clenched, the knuckles showing white. "We have to fight. The alternative is to die." He looked at the navigator. "It's up to you," he said. "You and the captain. There's nothing I can do."

"You can pray," said Nimino softly. "You can always do that."

Lallia stirred as Dumarest entered the cabin, lifting her arms as he turned on the light. "Earl, my darling. How did you know I wanted you?"

He made no comment, standing watching her, cups of basic in his hands. Sleep had washed the lines of fatigue from her face, lessened the heavy pallor, so that lying in the aureole of her hair she looked very young and very helpless. He stooped and set down the cups, feeling her arms close around him, the warm scent of her breath against his cheek.

"Come to me, lover. Come to me now."

"You'd better drink this," he said. "I want you to swallow as much basic as you can hold."

"Aren't I fat enough for you, lover?" She lost her smile

as she saw his face. "Earl! Something's wrong! What is it?"

"We're going to crash," he said flatly. "And I think it will be soon."

"Crash?"

"The generators are failing. Sheyan did all he could but it wasn't enough. Now he's trying to get us down all in one piece."

He looked at the woman and thought of the captain, of Sheyan's innate fear as he had been woken from the comfort of his symbiote, his steely acceptance of what had to be done. The generators had defeated him, now he was in the control room, slumped in his big chair, doing what the mechanisms around him could no longer do.

For they worked by rigid patterns governed by the steady progress of the ship. That progress was no longer steady, random forces increasing the velocity by multiplying factors, the gravity fields of close-set suns affecting the vessel in unexpected ways. Like a blind man threading a needle through a mass of electrified wire Sheyan was guiding the *Moray* through destructive energies. Their lives depended on his skill.

"I've spoken to Yalung," said Dumarest. "He knows what to do. Now I want you to do it. Eat as much as you can—food may be hard to find after we land. Wear as much as you can; the landing may be rough and we may have to leave the ship fast. Stay in this cabin and fasten the restraints. And pray," he added, remembering Nimino's advice. "For all we know it could help."

"Paraphysical forces working on an unaccepted plane of energy," she said evenly. "But, if we don't accept it, how can it affect us?"

"An apple may not accept the concept of gravity," he said. "But it falls just the same."

Lallia took a cup of basic, drank and looked thoughtfully into the empty container. "Prayer," she said. "I've done enough of it in the past. When I was a girl I prayed all the time for someone to take me away from the farm. Do you know what it's like working on a farm? We had no machines so I had to be up well before dawn and didn't get to bed until long after dark. The best I could hope for was for some man to marry me and take me back to his place and there work me to death. Well, that didn't happen. A young aristo saw me while out hunting and liked the way

I was built. I played up to him and he enjoyed his new toy. By the time he had tired of me I was safe off the farm." She looked at Dumarest. "Safe but in trouble. Rochis isn't a gentle world and an unprotected woman is anyone's sport. Do I have to tell you what happened then?"

Dumarest took the empty cup from her hand. "You don't have to tell me anything. The past doesn't matter."

"No," she said, and drew a deep breath. "Let's just say that I've knocked around. Anyway, I moved on the first ship I could get. I guess I've been moving ever since. Moving and looking for a thing called happiness. It isn't easy to find."

Dumarest handed her another cup of basic. "Drink this."

"I'll drink it." Her eyes were bright as she searched his face. "Earl! Do you know what I'm trying to say?"

"Drink your basic."

"To hell with it!" She slammed the cup down and circled him with her arms. "I'm telling you that I love you. That I've never known what love was before. That I can die happy knowing that we are together."

Dumarest lifted his hand and stroked the rich mass of her hair. He knew what she wanted him to say. "I love you, Lallia."

"You mean that?" Her arms tightened, pressed him close. "You really mean it?"

"I mean it."

"Then I've found it," she said. "Happiness, I mean. Earl, you'll never regret it. I'll be all the woman you could ever want. I'll—" She broke off as the ship gave a sudden lurch. "Earl?"

"It's nothing," he said quickly. "Opposed energies, perhaps, or the touch of atmosphere. Hurry now, do as I told you."

He left the cabin as the ship jerked again, the fabric shrilling as if the *Moray* was in actual, physical pain.

IX

THEY LANDED badly, hitting a range of low hills, bouncing over rock and scree, tearing a broad swathe through snow-laden trees before coming to a halt at the bottom of a shallow ravine. From the plateau beyond Nimino looked back at the column of smoke which marked the funeral pyre of the *Moray*.

"My books," he said. "My holy objects and sacred charms. Gone, all of them."

"They served their purpose," said Dumarest. "At least you are still alive." He glanced to where Yalung and the woman stood, shapeless in bundled garments, ankle-deep in azure snow. "We are alive," he corrected. "Your prayers and supplications must have been effective."

But not for the ship and not for its captain. Sheyan was dead, his blood and flesh mingled with the metal of the crushed vessel, charring now beneath the searing heat of released energies.

Yalung stirred, stamping his feet in the freezing snow. "Where are we?" he demanded. "What is the name of this world?"

"Shrine."

Dumarest looked at the navigator, remembering those he had seen at the carnival. "Then there is a settlement here. Ships and men to aid us."

Nimino shook his head. "No settlement, Earl. Shrine is a peculiar world. It is a place which is regarded by many as being holy. They come here hoping for a miracle to cure their deformities and many have their hopes realized. There is a sacred place protected by strange guardians. Ships call and leave but there is no town and no commerce."

Lallia said, "How do you know all this?"

"I was here once, many years ago, soon after I entered the Web. Often I suggested to Sheyan that he use the *Moray* as a pilgrim vessel but always he refused. The vessel was too small, the cost of conversion too high; a larger crew would have been needed together with medical personnel." Nimino looked to where the column of smoke climbed into the violet sky. "Well, he is here now and will stay here. The manipulations of fate often contain a strange irony."

"You helped him plot the course," said Dumarest. "What happened towards the end? Did he try to land near the settlement?"

"I told you, my friend, there is no settlement." The navigator beat his hands together, vapor pluming from his mouth. "And I left him long before we hit the atmosphere. But he would have tried to land us close to the field. He was a good captain," he added. "But for him we would still be in space, drifting wreckage or fused metal, we could even have fallen into a sun. He gave us life."

Dumarest looked at the sky, the surrounding terrain. The feeling of impotent helplessness of the past few hours was over now that he was back among familiar dangers. Cold and hunger and the peril of beasts. The need to survive and to escape from their present situation.

He glanced at the sky again. The sun was small, a ball of flaring orange rimmed with the inevitable corona, hanging low in a bowl of violet. The ground towards the hills was thick with snow, the soft carpeting broken by shrubs and mounded trees. Turning he looked towards the plateau. The snow continued, broken in the far distance by unfamiliar trees. They were tall and bulbous, set wide apart and each ringed with a circle of darkness. Beyond them the air held a peculiar shimmer.

Lallia shivered as a rising wind blew azure flecks into her face. "Earl, I'm cold."

Dumarest ignored the comment. To Nimino he said, "You were here before. What is the weather like? How low does the temperature fall?"

"I was at the sacred place," said the navigator. "Not out in the wilds. There the temperature is that of blood."

Warm air rising to meet upper layers of frigid cold would produce such a shimmer as lay beyond the trees. And Sheyan would have tried to put them down close. It was possible and yet, how in this wilderness could a place be so warm?

The wind strengthened a little, a flurry of snow streaming from the hills like azure smoke from a fire thick with ash.

"We had best find shelter," said Yalung. "The sun is setting and the cold will increase." He looked at the column of smoke, bent now, a ragged plume marring the sky. "The trees, perhaps?"

The shimmer lay beyond, it was the right direction.

"Yes," said Dumarest. "The trees."

They were further than he had guessed. In the clear air distance was hard to judge and it was growing dark by the time they reached the vicinity of the unfamiliar growths. He paused as they neared them, looking up at the soaring trees, alert for signs of aerial life. He saw nothing. Only the bulbous trunks spiked with a multitude of bristlelike protuberances. Leaves, he thought, or branches, or protective spines like those on a cactus. The dark rings beneath them were areas clear of snow, a thick, springy grass showing a dull brown in the fading light.

"Please, Earl." Lallia was shaking with the cold, the thick mane of her hair coated with azure flecks borne by the wind. "Can't we find somewhere to stay, build a fire, perhaps?"

"We could get behind a tree," suggested Yalung. The dealer's voice was even, he did not appear to feel the cold. "At least it would protect us from the wind."

Dumarest hesitated, caution prickling his nerves. There was a stillness about the forest he did not like. There should have been underbrush, birds, small animals, perhaps. There should have been the feel of life instead of the eerie stillness as if a giant animal were holding its breath and crouching ready to spring.

"A fire," said Nimino. He blew on his hands, his dark skin puckered with the cold. "Always man has found comfort in the leaping dance of a flame. I will gather wood while you select a place to rest." He was gone before Dumarest could object, his figure small against the bole of a soaring giant.

He jerked as something exploded.

It was a short, harsh sound like the vicious crack of a whip. Nimino stumbled and fell to roll on the dark mat of the grass. Dumarest caught Lallia as she went to run towards him.

"Wait!"

"But, Earl, he tripped and fell. He could be hurt."

"He didn't trip." Dumarest narrowed his eyes as he examined the tree. "If he did he will rise. Yalung, that explosion, did you hear it?"

"It sounded like the snapping of a branch," said the dealer slowly. "I think it came from the tree."

It came again as they watched, the hard, snapping sound accompanied by the flash of something dark which hit the ground close to where Nimino rolled in pain. Dumarest shouted towards the navigator.

"Don't move! Stay as you are!"

He ran forward as he shouted, head lowered, shoulders high. The cracking explosion came again as he reached the edge of the dark area and he sprang aside as a dozen shafts spined the place where he had been. More explosions echoed from the trees as he stopped, picked up the navigator and, cradling him in his arms, ran from the vicinity of the tree.

Something slammed into his back, his legs and arms, the impact accompanied by more vicious crackings. They ceased as he rejoined the others.

"The tree," said Yalung. "It fired spines at you. I saw the puffs against the bole."

"Earl!" said Lallia. "You were hit!"

Hit but not harmed, the spines had failed to penetrate the mesh buried within the plastic of his clothing. Nimino hadn't been as lucky. A half-dozen spines had hit his torso, finger-thick and covered with pointed scales. Dumarest touched one and felt the sting of poison. Even if they hadn't hit a vital part the navigator was as good as dead.

A defense mechanism, he thought. The trees protecting themselves or using the fired spines to bring down game so as to nourish their roots.

"Earl!" Nimino writhed in his agony, sweat beading his face. "Earl!"

"It's all right," said Dumarest. He lifted his right hand and rested the fingers on the navigator's throat. A pressure on the carotids and the man would pass quickly into unconsciousness and painless death.

"No!" Nimino twisted, one hand rising to knock away the fingers. "Not that, Earl. I want to see it coming. Meet it face to face."

He coughed and wiped his mouth, looking at the red bright against the darkness of his hand.

"It burns," he said. "God, how it burns!" His hand reached for Dumarest's, found it, tightened. "Earl, do you think I'll have to pay for Claude? Start again at the very beginning? It's such a long, hard climb, Earl. So long. Will I ever reach the Ultimate?"

"Yes," said Dumarest quietly. "You're going to it now. You won't have to pay for Claude. You killed him in order to save my life."

"Yes," said Nimino. He coughed again, blood staining his lips and chin. "Earl, I lied to you. About Earth. I said I didn't know anything about it. I lied."

"You know where it is?" Dumarest stooped close to the dying man, his eyes intent. "How I can find it?"

"Not where it is. But in the old books, the religious works, they talk of it." Nimino's voice faded, became a liquid gurgling. "In the beginning God created the heaven and the earth," he said. "The Earth, Earl! And there is more. In the Rhamda Veda it says: 'From terror did the people fly and they did scatter themselves in the heavens.' Terror, Earl, or Terra? I have thought much about it since you joined the *Moray*." He coughed again and his voice became clearer. "Find the Original People, Earl. They hold secret knowledge and legends born in ancient days. The Original People."

"A sect?" Dumarest gripped the hand within his own. "What are they, Nimino? A religious sect?"

"Yes, Earl. They will tell you of the Dog Star and the Plow, the magic signs of the zodiac. Where you can see them that is where you will find Earth. They—" The navigator broke off, his eyes widening as he stared past Dumarest. "You!" he gasped. "But how—"

Dumarest turned. Behind him was nothing but a mist of swirling snow, azure flecks caught and spun in the wind, ghostly against the darkening sky. He looked back. Nimino's eyes were still open, still holding an expression of incredulity, but the blood no longer seeped from his parted lips. As he watched a thin patina of azure snow began to cover the dead face.

Gently he closed the staring eyes.

"He's gone?" Lallia was a dim bulk at his side as he rose to his feet. "Earl, is he dead?"

"He was talking," said Yalung. "What did he say?"

"Nothing of importance," said Dumarest. "He was rambling."

"I thought he might have told us how to get through the trees." The dealer sounded irritable. "He was here once before."

"And saw nothing," reminded Dumarest. "And he could know nothing of the trees or he would not have run towards them." He looked at the sky, the shadowed glades. "We'll have to try and go around them. Perhaps there is a path."

For two days they walked beside the forest, slaking their thirst on snow and sleeping huddled together for warmth. At dawn on the third day Dumarest announced his decision.

"As far as I can tell these trees completely surround the place we have to reach. Therefore we have to go through them."

"And end like the navigator?" Yalung looked at the unbroken ranks of trees.

"There could be a way." Dumarest pointed. "See? The grass areas around the trees do not completely meet. I have been watching and all are the same. My guess is that the grass is a form of symbiote. The trees kill game and the grass devours it, in turn feeding the tree and at the same time acting as a sort of trigger mechanism for the spines." He picked up a small boulder. "Watch!"

Explosions cracked the air as the mass of stone fell among the grass of one of the areas. A dozen shafts splintered on the target.

"Now watch this." Again Dumarest threw a large stone, this time on the narrow strip of snow between two of the trees. Nothing happened.

"I see what you mean," said Lallia. "But suppose it gets dark before we pass through the forest?"

"We sleep and continue the next day."

"And if that isn't enough?"

"We have no choice," said Yalung before Dumarest could answer. "Here we shall freeze, or starve. Already we are weakening." He turned his round, yellow face away from the wind. "If you lead I shall follow."

It was like treading an intricate maze. No path was straight and all followed circles so that to progress a mile they had to walk four. And, always, Dumarest was conscious of the danger of getting lost.

His guides were the sun and the strange shimmer in the air beyond the trees. The sun moved across the sky but the shimmer did not and, fortunately, the trees were wide-spaced enough to allow fairly good vision. Even so the going was hard. The eerie silence of the forest began to play on their nerves and moving shadows gave the impression of watchful menace.

The wind fell and the snow vanished. Night caught them and they took turns to sleep, one watching while the others sprawled in the narrow margin of safety. With the dawn came a raging thirst adding to the weakness caused by cold and lack of food. The cold could be combated by exertion, but the thirst could not. Twice Yalung called a sharp warning as Lallia staggered and almost left the path. The third time Dumarest halted and looked into the strained lines of her face.

"I'm sorry, Earl," she said. "I couldn't help it. It's got so that I seem to be walking in a dream." She looked around, shuddering. "It's so damn quiet. If only something would make a noise. And," she added with feeling, "if only there was something to drink."

"Stay here." Dumarest turned and walked on to the next area of grass. Dropping he reached out with his boot and scraped it towards him. As he tore at the grass explosions blasted the air and shafts rained towards him. His boots were strong and, like his pants, resisted penetration. Picking up the clump of grass he returned to the others. "Chew on this," he said. "It might help."

Dubiously Lallia took the tangled vegetation. It was a mass of thick, juicy strands, the ends seeping where it had broken away. Sight of the liquid inflamed her thirst and she thrust some of the grass into her mouth, chewing and swallowing, sap staining her lips as she helped herself to more.

"It's good," she said. "Have some."

Yalung said, quietly, "Thank you, no. I can continue for a while yet."

"Earl?"

"Later, maybe. Now stick to the path and don't start daydreaming."

They reached the edge of the forest as the sun kissed the horizon, long shadows streaming from the ranked trees and hiding the terrain so that they were clear long before they realized it. Now they walked on close-cropped grass dotted with low bushes, bearing flame-colored berries and thorned leaves. A tiny lake yielded water of crystal clarity, cold but more delicious than wine. Later Dumarest managed to kill a small animal, spearing it with his knife at thirty feet, cleaning the beast and jointing it, using the fur to wipe the blade.

Chewing on the raw gobbets of meat they walked on to where the shimmer hung against the blossoming stars.

They were few and Dumarest looked at them with a strange nostalgia. So had the stars looked from Earth when he had been very young. Not the shimmer and glare so common in and close to the Center, but a scatter of burning points separated by wide expanses of darkness. They had formed patterns, those stars, and the broad swath of the galactic lens had traced a shining path across the heavens. But they had been scattered by distance and not, as the stars in the Web, by the cloud of shielding dust.

"Look," said Yalung softly. "A ship."

It fell wreathed in the misty blue of its field, a tiny mote incredibly far, falling as a meteor to a point beyond the horizon. Landing at the sacred place which, so Nimino had said, was protected by strange guardians. The trees? Dumarest didn't think so. They were guardians of a kind but not the ones the navigator had meant.

He paused as a thin trilling stirred the air, the ghostly echoes of a crystal chime, sounding high and shrill and far away.

A sweet and soulful sound, unbearably poignant, arousing memories better left undisturbed.

"Earl!" Lallia came close to him and caught his arm. "Earl, what was that?"

It came again as she fell silent, thin, hurtfully pure. A third time and then the night settled into unbroken silence.

"A signal," said Yalung thoughtfully. "It must have sounded when the ship landed. A summons, perhaps?" He sucked in his breath with an audible hiss. "Look! The sky!"

Ahead, where the shimmer had disturbed the cold beauty of the stars, leaped a vibrant cone of coruscating brilliance. It lasted for perhaps half a minute and then, as abruptly as it had come, was gone.

The ship left at dawn. Lallia watched as it rose, tiny in the distance, the blue mist of its field almost lost against the brightening sky. Her face was haggard as she looked at Dumarest.

"Earl! We're too late! It's gone!"

"There will be others," he said. "Ships must come here all the time."

"They come," agreed Yalung. "But will they take any who ask for passage? Will they be allowed to? This is a strange world."

He halted, brooding as he studied the sky. They had been walking for hours, using the stars as a guide, avoiding the thorned bushes more by instinct than actual sight. They had found no more lakes and there had been no more game.

"How much further do you think we have to go?"

"A long way," said Dumarest. The ship had been small, their progress of the night had been negligible, the faint shimmer in the sky seemed no closer. "A week, perhaps, even longer, but we'll get there in the end."

"If we can stay alive that long." Fatigue had made the woman sharp. "There's something crazy about this place. We've been walking for miles and seem no closer now than we did at the start. Maybe we'll never get closer. We could be moving in a giant circle."

"No," said Dumarest. "Not that."

"Then why are we so far? We—" She broke off and then said, wonderingly. "Look, Earl. Birds."

"The first we have seen," said Yalung quietly. "But —are they birds?"

They came from the direction in which they were heading, winged motes against the sky, wheeling and circling before swooping down at the travelers. There was something odd about them. Dumarest watched as they came, eyes like jewels and feathers rustling like metal, wide wings throwing shadows on the ground. They were big, their wings extended fully twenty feet, their bodies as long as the height of a man. Their beaks were glinting spears and their clawed feet stretched as if to engulf barrels. From halfway down their bodies stretched limbs ending in long, prehensile fingerlike claws. Three of them landed just ahead, the rest circling watchfully above.

The guardians?

Dumarest studied them as they stood, wings folded, apparently waiting. Mutated biological mechanisms, he thought, fed on a diet heavy in metallic oxides and silicon. That would account for the rasping of the feathers, the sparkling gleam of bone and scale. Multilimbed creatures produced in order to fly, to walk, to grip and tear. Or perhaps they were a natural sport of this peculiar world. It didn't matter. To resist them would be suicide.

"They are barring our path," said Yalung. "A warning?"

"We can't turn back!" Lallia's voice held near-hysteria. "Earl, we can't turn back!"

Dumarest looked at the other winged shapes circling overhead. Reenforcements, perhaps, if they should somehow manage to overcome the three ahead. With lasers they could have killed them all but they had no weapons aside from his knife. And, even if they could have destroyed the birds, would that end their danger?

Slowly he walked forward to stand before the three silent images. They were like statues of burnished metal and shining crystal, the idols of some ancient temple, utterly remote from human comprehension. The light of the rising sun shone redly from their eyes, beyond them the enigmatic shimmer quivered in the silent air.

Dumarest said, "We are survivors of a wrecked vessel. We wish to go to the field, there to obtain passage from this world."

A voice, cold, emotionless, echoed wordlessly in his mind, in the minds of them all.

"It is understood. Do not resist."

Wings lifted, flexed as they beat the air, the rustle of feathers a tintinnabulation. Lallia gasped as she was picked from the ground, hair flying as she turned in the grip of prehensile fingers. Yalung was next, his yellow face impassive as he was carried away. Dumarest followed, feeling the firm grip on his body, the sighing rush of air past his face. Around the three the other birds formed an escort as they first climbed then leveled in whispering flight.

Far below the ground swept past like an unrolling carpet. The bushed plain, dotted with tiny lakes few and far between. A circle of spine-bearing trees, a swampy morass succulent with livid grasses steaming with oozing mud, a rearing mound of stone surrounding a mass of scree and then, finally, a thick growth of timber at the side of which rested the unmistakable expanse of a landing field.

It swelled as they plummeted towards it, the bare ground torn and scarred from the impact of tremendous energies, tiny figures working to level the surface. Dumarest looked at them as the ground hit his feet and the bird which had carried him winged away. They were simple creatures with wide jaws and spadelike forepaws, clawed feet and a flat tail. Where they passed freshly turned soil rested flat and smooth behind them.

He lifted his eyes. The perimeter fence was high and stronger than any he had previously seen. A mesh of thick bars fifty feet high, so close that it was almost a solid wall. A single gate broke it where it faced the expanse of timber beyond.

As Dumarest watched it opened and a figure passed through.

"God!" Lallia's voice was a whisper at his side. "Earl, what is it?"

"A guardian." Yalung had no doubt. "One of those the navigator mentioned. It can be nothing else."

From the tip of the cowl to the hem of the trailing robe the figure was twelve feet tall, incredibly broad, the figure bulking beneath the muffling robe of glinting metallic fiber. The face was shadow in which transient gleams of variegated color flashed and died in winking splendor. The hands, if the creature had hands, were hidden in wide sleeves. There were no signs of feet or locomotive appendages.

Dumarest had the impression that the thing was entirely unhuman. That the robe was worn for concealment and that the figure bulking beneath was completely alien.

Again the cold, emotionless voice echoed wordlessly in his mind.

"You have come to the Place. You are welcome."

"Thank you," said Dumarest quickly before the others could answer. "We had misfortune. Our vessel crashed on some hills far from here. It was kind of you to send your servants to give us aid."

The birds could be nothing else. They shared the alienness of the tall figure but they could not be the masters. Nothing could be the master of the enigmatic being which stood before them. It was wrapped in an aura of power almost as tangible as the metallic robe covering its body.

Yalung stirred and said, "We require little. Some food and water while we wait for the arrival of a ship to carry us from this world."

Lallia added, "And somewhere to bathe. Is that possible?"

Colored sparkles flashed and died in the shadow of the cowl.

"In the Place all things are possible. Ask and you shall be given."

The figure turned and glided towards the open gate, the mystery of the area beyond. Dumarest followed, the others just behind.

He stepped into a cathedral.

X

It WAS A place of mystery and awe-inspiring majesty, the still air hanging like incense, tiny motes of dust glinting in the shadowed sunlight like tiny candles set before incredible altars. Dumarest felt Yalung bump into him, heard Lallia's low voice at his side.

"Earl," she said. "It's beautiful!"

A wide avenue stretched before them, floored with soft, close-cropped grass and flanked by the slender boles of soaring trees. They reared like columns, a tuft of branches high overhead fanning to meet and form a natural arch through which streamed the ruby light of the sun. Ahead, shadowed in the distance, more columns sprang from the tended soil, circling a clearing about an indistinguishable structure, a boulder, perhaps, an outcrop of natural stone wreathed and hung with living garlands.

Down the avenue, diminished in the distance, the tall figure of the strange Guardian, seemed to flicker and then to abruptly vanish.

Slowly Dumarest walked down the avenue.

It was the pilgrim's way, he guessed, the path which those seeking the miracle of healing followed as they made their way to the holy place. There would be attendants to carry those unable to walk, others to help those who could barely stand, a motley thronging of deformity and pain each united by a common hope. But now there was nothing but the three of them, the quiet susurration of their footsteps on the springy grass, the sound of their breathing.

And it was warm, the temperature that of living blood. "Earl." Lallia turned to him, her face beaded with perspiration. "I can't stand this heat. I've got to get rid of these clothes."

They stripped at one side of the avenue, shedding the extra, bulky garments they had worn on leaving the ship and then, the woman in her iridescent dress, Yalung in his yellow and black, Dumarest in his neutral gray, continued down the path between the trees.

How many had preceded them, thought Dumarest. How long had these trees grown, shaped by careful tending, planted and culled, bred and trained? How many ships had dropped from the skies with their loads of misery and hope? The place reeked of sanctity, of devotion and supplication. The trees had absorbed the emotions of the incalculable number of pilgrims who had visited Shrine and followed the guardian into the holy place. Holy because they had made it so? Or holy because here, in this spot, something beyond the physical experience of men had stopped and left its mark?

Faith, he thought. Here, surely, if a man had faith miracles could happen.

"Earl, look!"

Lallia's whisper was loud in the brooding stillness. She had advanced a little and now stood at the edge of the clearing in which stood the mysterious object. It was no clearer than it had been when seen from far down the avenue. The woman stood beside a heap of something beneath a wide awning of natural growth. A chapel made by leafy branches. It was brimming with articles of price.

Fine fabric, precious metal, cunning fabrications of metal and wood and blazing ceramics. The glint of gems and gold and the crystal perfection of faceted glass. All intermingled with less rare objects, a cloak, a cane, a visored helm, the leather of belts and the scaled skins of serpents, sacks of spices and seed and pleasing aromatics. The roll of charts, maps, paintings of a hundred different schools.

"Votive offerings," said Yalung softly. "Things given in appreciation and gratitude. A fortune beyond the dreams of avarice on any of a million worlds."

And there were more. The chapels surrounded the clearing and all contained a heap of similar items. Lallia paused, looking at a scatter of ancient books.

She touched one and her face stiffened with psychic shock.

"Earl!" she whispered. "It's so old, old! There is hope and a terrible fear and—and—"

He caught her as she slumped, the book falling from her hand. It fell open and he had a glimpse of strange figures, of lines and tabulated numerations, of diagrams and vaguely familiar symbols.

Yalung picked it up, closed it, returned it to the heap. Quietly he said, "How is the girl?"

"I'm all right." Lallia straightened from Dumarest's arms and shook her head as if to clear it of mist. "It was just that —Earl, the book is so old!"

An ancient book. A stellar almanac, perhaps. A pre-Center-orientated navigational manual. In this place anything was possible.

He reached for it, arresting his hand as a familiar voice echoed in his mind.

"Come."

Dumarest looked up. The strange guardian stood to one side. Watching? It was hard to tell if the figure had a face or eyes at all but the enigmatic flickering in the shadow of the cowl gave the impression of senses more finely tuned than those owned by ordinary men.

"The Place awaits. Go to it. Place your hands on it. This is the rule."

"The guardian means that object in the middle of the clearing," said Yalung. He sounded dubious. "I am not sure that we should do as he directs."

"Have we any choice?" Lallia smiled. "And I want a bath. Remember what was promised? Ask and you will be given. Anyway, what have we to lose?"

Life, thought Dumarest. Sanity, our health, perhaps. Who can tell?

But he followed her across the clearing.

The mound was high, larger than he had at first supposed, a vine-draped mass protruding from the neatly kept grass. A special grass, he thought, to withstand the weight of the thousands who must come here. As the mound had to be something special also. A strangely-shaped fragment of stone, perhaps, a meteor even, a thing to which had become attached a tremendous superstition. Or did naked belief make its own holiness? Could faith convert inanimate matter into a healing being?

Nimino could have answered, but the navigator was dead. Coughing out his life in order to fulfill a prophecy that he would achieve great knowledge in a cloud of dust. The Web was such a cloud and what greater knowledge could come to a man than that of what happened after death?

Dumarest shook his head, annoyed at his own introspection, wondering what had sent his thoughts on such a path. The influence of the place, he thought. The mystery and enchantment of it. The brooding majesty and overwhelming sense of sanctity. There was magic in the air, perhaps the emanations of the trees, the invisible vapors released by the grass, subtle drugs to fog the senses and open wide the vistas of the mind. But that again was sheer speculation.

He concentrated on the mound.

There was an oddity about it as there had been about the birds, as there was about the guardian. A peculiar sense of alienness as if it did not belong to this world and never had. Dumarest narrowed his eyes, tilting his head so as to sharpen his vision, probing beneath the obvious to seek the underlying truth. It probably was simply a mound but there was an oddity here, a peculiar something there, a slight distortion just above the line of sight. And then, suddenly, as if he were looking at an optical illusion in which one image was hidden within another, details grew clear.

The mound was no heap of vine-covered stone.

It was the wreckage of a manufactured artifact.

He blinked but there was no mistake. Warped and crushed as it was, misshapen and unfamiliar, he could still make out the angles and curves of vanes, the ridges of corrugations, plates and sheets of metal all overlaid with grime and a patina of soil from which grew shielding vines.

Or were they, too, disguised? Cables, perhaps, flexible conduits, pipes which had burst like entrails from the body of the artifact?

Dumarest heard the sharp intake of Yalung's breath and wondered if the dealer in precious stones had also penetrated the illusion. And Lallia? He glanced at her, noting the smoothness of her face, the rapt expression in her eyes. She looked like a little girl as she stood before the mound, a child basking in the promise of comfort and warmth and security. She had once prayed, he remembered, and all who pray must have some belief in a higher power. Did she imagine that she stood before the abode of such a being?

"Lallia," he called softly. "Wait."

She halted and turned, smiling, the full richness of her lips red against the whiteness of her skin. "Why, Earl?"

"It would be wise to wait," said Yalung. "If the guardian will allow it." He glanced to where the tall figure stood at the edge of the clearing, as immobile as a statue. "The mound is not quite what it seems."

"Does it matter?" She shrugged, suddenly impatient. "What's the matter with you two? It's only a gesture. We aren't sick or ill and if they can come here and touch it without harm what have we to fear? Anyway I'm curious to see whether or not I get my bath."

She held out her hands, again smiling.

"Come on, Earl. Come on the pair of you. Let's touch it together."

For a moment Dumarest hesitated, then reached for her hand. After all, what could there be to fear?

Together the three of them rested their hands on the fabric of the Place.

Nothing, thought Dumarest. He felt the touch of harshness beneath his palms, saw the grain of dirt and soil before his eyes. A patina built over how long? Centuries, certainly, thousands of years, perhaps, wind-blown dust, rain, the slow, relentless attrition of the years. But why hadn't the metal beneath the dirt yielded to the impact of time?

And who had originally built it?

And why?

He heard the soft movement of Yalung's body as the man shifted his feet. Lallia was breathing quietly, hands and cheek pressed against the mound, eyes closed as if she were making a secret wish. Entering into the spirit of the thing, perhaps. Acting as if she were a genuine pilgrim seeking a miracle. And, if one came, just what would the effect be?

Dumarest thought he knew. Faith healing was nothing unusual. Many had the gift and could heal with a touch, it was merely another facet of the paraphysical sciences revealed in the talents of various sensitives. In effect they were simply catalysts directing the body to repair itself from the blueprint inherent in every molecule of D.N.A. If a machine could be developed to do the same thing then every city would have its Shrine. Its holy spot. Its Place.

He smiled and closed his eyes, willing to play the game to the full, trying to feel as a genuine pilgrim would feel. If he had been sick or crippled he would have concentrated on his infirmity.

Instead he could only think of Earth.

Earth, the planet which had become lost to him, the need to find which had become an aching obsession. Could a man be whole without a home? And could a man who was not whole be considered other than as a cripple? Deformities were not always of the flesh and bone. And what was loss but a deformity of the mind?

A moment of peculiar, subconscious strain and then abruptly, Dumarest saw a picture in his mind.

It was shining with bright splendor, a flattened disc with vaguely spiral arms, a pattern composed of a myriad of glowing points, hazes, somber patches of ebon and traces of luminous cloud. Instinctively he knew what it was. The galactic lens as seen from above and to one side.

In it one tiny fleck shone with blazing ruby fire.

It was well from the Center, lying in a distant arm of the spiral, a lonely place among few and scattered stars but he knew exactly what it was.

Home.

The planet for which he had been searching for too long. The world which had given him birth. Earth.

And he knew now almost exactly where to look for it.

Almost, for the galaxy was vast and the stars innumerable and no one brain can hold the complexity of an island universe. But the sector was there, the approximate position, the direction from the Center. It would be enough.

Dumarest jerked as the picture vanished, an eerie tension of his nerves, a something in his brain as if fingers of mist had drawn themselves across the naked cortex and with the touch had taken something of himself. Opening his eyes he stared at the material before him. It looked exactly the same, but as he watched he saw a fragile glow of light, a vague sparkle of quickly vanished luminescence.

To one side Yalung groaned, falling to sit upright blinking and shaking his head.

"Strange," he said thickly. "So strange. And I feel now now discomfort. My thirst has gone, my hunger. But how?"

Dumarest frowned, flexing his back and shoulders. The nagging discomfort of his barely healed wounds had totally vanished and he too felt neither hunger or thirst. Lallia?

She lay sprawled on the grass, hands touching the mound, her face a strained mask of torment. As Dumarest watched, it contorted and writhed, adopting a snarling mask of hideous aspect. Then it relaxed to reveal the familiar planes and contours.

"Lallia!" He knelt at her side, touching her skin, the pulse in her throat. Her muscles were like iron.

"No!" she screamed as he tried to pull her hands from the mound. "No!" and then, quieter, "Dear God, how long, how old!"

Yalung rose, a yellow shadow to kneel at her far side. "She is ill," he said. "A fit perhaps?"

It was no fit, not unless psychic shock could be called that. Too late Dumarest remembered her wild talent, the ability to remember the past of any object she touched. The ancient book should have warned him but he had been engrossed in the possibility that it could help in his search. He had not thought of the possibility that the mound could hold a similar danger. Not even when he had recognized it as an artifact.

And now it was too late for regret.

"Earl!" She writhed again, sensing an agonizing past, the dusty span of painful years. "Three suns," she whispered. "A fault in the engines. Suspended animation and millennia of travel. Such darkness and chill and then the dust and the wakening. Too late. The crash and the waiting, the endless waiting." She twisted and moaned, midnight hair wreathed on the grass. "It's alive, Earl. Still alive. Waiting and hoping. Such forlorn longing, Earl!"

She stiffened, and from the very pores of her skin seeped a lambent effulgence, a mist of luminescence which flowed down her arms to the material of the ancient wreck and, as it finally separated from her body, she sighed and totally relaxed.

"Is she dead?" Yalung's face was a yellow mask in the shadows.

Dumarest examined her body, heart pounding with the fear of what he might find. Relieved he sat back and looked at the other man.

"Not dead," he said. "Exhausted by tremendous psychic shock. You understand?"

"Yes," said Yalung. "I understand."

"All of it?" Dumarest glanced at the mound. "It is a wrecked spaceship. It came from God alone knows where, but I will guess that it was never made in our galaxy. And, somehow, something within it is still alive."

Crippled, perhaps, hurt, but still aware. For unguessed millennia it had lain within the vessel tended only by the repair mechanisms the ship had contained—and by the enigmatic guardians if there were more than one? It was possible, they could have bred the birds and the protoplasmic machines which tended the field and the Place itself. Or perhaps they were extensions of the entity within the ship, prosthetic devices governed by its intelligence. Who could begin to guess at the mental structure of an alien race?

And, by means of her talent, Lallia had contacted it. She had sent a part of her mentality back down through the ages, barely understanding, capable only of feeling the terrible shock and despair, the age-long time it had traversed the endless dark, the indescribable alienness of its emotions as it waited and waited for years without end.

For rescue, perhaps? For death? For someone to come who would know and understand?

Dumarest looked at the mound and then back at the girl. She was not dead and that was the important thing. She would lie in a coma for a while and then wake as she had back on the *Moray*, alive and sane and well. They would still have a future.

Stooping he lifted her in his arms.

"Where are you taking her?" Yalung glanced around the clearing then down the length of the avenue to the gate and high fence at the end. "Perhaps close to the landing field would be best. Anywhere away from this mound which seems to have distressed her."

Away from the ancient vessel, the enigmatic guardian who

stood, still immobile, dancing flickers gleaming from the shadow of its cowl. Away from the brooding stillness of the Place, the psychic influences which seemed to pervade the very grass and trees.

Dumarest began to walk down the wide avenue.

He staggered and frowned. The girl was not that heavy and he felt strong enough. Strong but suddenly weary as if he had suffered some tremendous strain and fatigue was the natural aftermath. Yalung tripped and almost fell, shaking his head as he recovered his balance.

"I am fatigued," he said. "Filled with the desire to sleep. At the end of the avenue, perhaps? There is open space between the trees."

He led the way, falling to sprawl on the grass as Dumarest gently set down the body of the girl. For a long moment he stared at her, drinking in the smooth beauty of her face, the lustrous waterfall of her hair. She stirred a little sighing like a child in a pleasant dream, full lips parted to breathe his name.

"Earl, my darling. I love you so very much."

He moved a coil of hair from her cheek and arranged her limbs so as to avoid later cramps then, barely able to keep open his eyes, lay down beside her on the soft and yielding turf.

He fell asleep immediately, falling into a dreamless, timeless oblivion.

When he woke Lallia was dead.

XI

SHE LOOKED very small and helpless as she lay on the grass. She rested on her side, the long curves of her thighs white beneath the hem of her dress, the dark tresses of her hair covering cheek and throat. One arm was lifted, the palm close to her mouth, the other rested in her lap. She looked as if she would wake at a touch, a word, springing to her feet, red lips smiling, warm flesh pulsing with the desire of life, but he had tried both word and touch and she was dead.

"She could not have survived the psychic shock she received at the mound," said Yalung quietly. He stood beside Dumarest looking down at the kneeling man, the dead body of the girl. "It is unfortunate but it would appear to be the case."

"No," said Dumarest. "It wasn't that."

"How can you be sure?"

"I'm sure."

She had spoken his name, rising up from the deathlike coma of shock to drift into normal sleep, yielding to the strange fatigue which had gripped them all. Dumarest looked at the grass, the trees, lifting his face to search the soaring arch high above, the fading light of the sun. If she had died because of subtle emanations then why not all? The guardians, perhaps? But then, again, why kill the girl and not those with her? And how had she died? He could see no mark or injury, no fleck of blood from a minute puncture which would have betrayed the injection of poison from sting or needle.

Reaching out he caught the rounded chin and turned the dead face towards the sky. He stooped, bending his face close to the skin, moving so as to see it against the light. Faint against the marbled whiteness he could see the smudge of bruises against nostrils and mouth.

Rising he looked at Yalung. "You," he said. "You murdered her."

"You wrong me." Yalung raised his hands in denial. His eyes were wary in the yellow mask of his face. "Why do you say that? You have no proof."

"She was smothered to death by a hand which closed her nostrils and covered her mouth." Dumarest fought to control his rising anger. "I did not do it. We are the only humans in the vicinity. You must have woken earlier than I did and you killed the woman. But why? What harm had she done you?"

"None," admitted Yalung. He moved a step nearer to Dumarest, yellow and black rippling as he moved his arms, extending the broad spades of his hands. "But alive she was an inconvenience."

"You admit it?"

"But, of course. What point is there in denying the obvious?"

Dumarest moved, stooping, his hand flashing to the hilt of the knife in his boot, lifting the pointed, razor-edged steel. Sunlight gleamed from the blade as he swept it back and then forward, the point aimed at the other man's stomach.

Yalung sprang forward and to one side, his left hand

dropping to grasp the knife-wrist; twisting, his right hand jerking free the steel. As Dumarest struck at his throat he moved again, stepping to avoid the blow, the stiffened fingers of his left hand stabbing like blunted spears.

Dumarest staggered, fighting a red tide of agony, his right arm numbed and paralyzed.

"You are fast," said Yalung. "Very fast. But not fast enough to one who has trained on Kha." He looked at the knife and tossed it casually to one side. Dumarest watched its flight.

"You? A Kha'tung fighter?"

"You know of us?" Yalung's smile was a facial distortion without real meaning. "Can you imagine what it is like? For twenty years I trained on a high-gravity planet with pain as the constant reward for laggard reflexes. You should be proud that I was chosen. No lesser man would have been able to overcome you so easily."

He was confident but with justification. Fighting the pain of impacted nerves Dumarest studied the figure in yellow and black. The round plumpness wasn't the fat he had assumed but a thick layer of trained and hardened muscle. The broad hands, soft as they appeared, could smash timber and brick, stab deep into vital organs. A Kha'tung fighter was a deadly machine.

Dumarest said, "Why?"

"You are curious," said Yalung. "Well, we have time to spare until a ship arrives. He stepped close and stared into Dumarest's eyes. "Sit," he ordered, and pushed.

The blow was the thrust of an iron ram. Dumarest fell backwards, staggering, falling to roll on the soft grass. Awkwardly he sat upright, his left hand massaging his right arm. A random shaft of light caught the gem on his finger and turned it into ruby flame.

"The past," said Yalung. "Let us throw our minds back into time." He sat crossed legged, facing Dumarest at a safe distance of a dozen feet, his back towards the dead body of the girl. "Let us talk of names. Of Solis, of Brasque, of Kalin. I am sure that you remember Kalin."

"I remember."

"An unusual woman," said Yalung. "Most unusual. But let us start with Brasque. You never met him because he died before you reached Solis, but before he died he gave his sister the gift of life. Real life in a warm and healthy body. That secret he stole from the laboratory of the Cyclan. It must be returned."

Dumarest sat, patiently waiting, his left hand continuing its massage.

"The secret was that of an artificial symbiote named an affinity twin. It consists of fifteen units and the reversal of one unit makes it either subjective or dominant. Injected into the bloodstream it nestles in the rear of the cortex, meshes with the thalamus and takes control of the central nervous system. I need hardly tell you what that means."

The intelligence of a crippled body given active life in a healthy host. The ability of one brain to completely dominate another. Dumarest had good reason to know what it meant.

"No," he said. "You don't have to tell me."

"The path Brasque took has been followed and all possibilities of his passing the secret to others eliminated. The probability that he delivered the secret to his sister on Solis is one of the order of 99 percent—practical certainty. Investigations have proved that the secret is not on that planet so, logically, it must be elsewhere. Do you agree?"

"You talk like a cyber," said Dumarest. "A thing of flesh and blood, a machine, a creature devoid of the capability of emotion."

Yalung's eyes glittered in the round blandness of his face. "You think you insult me," he said. "Let me assure you that to be called a cyber is far from that. To belong to the Cyclan is not easy. To wear the scarlet robe is to be clad in honor."

Did the voice hold pride? Pride was an emotion and no cyber could feel anything other than pleasure in mental achievement. An operation on the sensory nerves leading to the brain removed all pain, hurt, anger, love, the pleasure to be found in food and wine, the caresses of women.

Dumarest eased himself a little, moving on the grass. "I follow your argument and admit your point."

"The rest is simple, a matter of extrapolating from known data. You were on Solis at the time. You were close to the sister of Brasque. You were given the gift of a ring. The probability of the ring holding the secret is in the order of 90 percent."

"And you killed Lallia for that?" Dumarest glanced towards the dead girl, then at the squatting figure before him. "I have the ring. Why not kill me and take it?"

"Because that would be illogical," said Yalung. "Too much

time has passed. You could have learned the secret or have changed the ring. To kill you would have been to lose a source of information for all time." He paused, eyes watchful. "The secret is a matter of the correct sequence of the molecular units composing the chain. There are fifteen units. Their nature is known. All that remains is to discover the order in which they must be united. But the task is not easy. If it were possible to test one combination every second it would take over four thousand years to test them all. And there are reasons why the Cyclan cannot wait. Good reasons. But now they need wait no longer."

"The ring is just what it seems," said Dumarest. "It contains no secret."

"I think that you lie. Twice I offered to buy it from you and each time you refused to sell. The price was high for such a bauble and your refusal convinced me that you were aware of its true worth." Yalung glanced once behind him as if sensing the presence of some entity, but the avenue and the space between the trees was deserted. "I should have had you safe on Aarn. I killed the thief who tried to rob you in the hotel. Normally the police would have arrested you and the ring would have come into my possession while you would have been kept safely in prison. But you were too quick. I could do nothing but follow you into the Web. Once in, I had no choice but to continue as I had begun."

An accident, thought Dumarest. The unpredictable workings of destiny. A primitive sense of danger and the quick grasping of an opportunity. Who could have predicted that one man would kill another at that exact place and time? Or that he would have been given the dead man's job?

Quietly he said, "And now?"

"You are my patient. A poor fool touched in the brain who is not responsible for what he says and what he does. I shall take passage on the next ship for us both and you will be drugged and bound for the entire journey. I have the means to charter the vessel if that will be necessary." Yalung slapped his belt. "My pouch of precious stones. Genuine jewels of high value. Ten times their worth will be mine when I have delivered you to the Cyclan."

Dumarest lifted his left hand from his right arm and looked at the ring. The impacted nerves had recovered a little but the arm still felt numb, was still unreliable. He raised his right hand and began to fumble with the ring.

"You want this," he said. "You had better take it."

His fingers were too awkward. He lifted the ring and held it between his teeth, pulling until it slipped free. It fell and he scrabbled for it, easing himself back over the grass. Picking it up with his right hand he held it so that it caught the light.

"If this contains such a valuable secret then perhaps you are selling it too cheap?"

"The bargain is satisfactory."

"We could make much more than you hope to gain. I know what the affinity twin can do. Together we could dominate a dozen worlds."

"And live for how long?" Yalung gestured his contempt. "You underestimate the power of the Cyclan. Should I try to play them false my death would be certain."

"All men die," said Dumarest flatly. "And all women." He glanced once at the body of the girl. "But not often does a man get such an opportunity as now lies within your grasp. You want money and power? I give it to you."

He threw the ring.

It spun high in the air, glittering, a thick band of gold holding a flat, rubylike stone. Yalung snatched at it as he would a fly, missed, and automatically turned to follow its flight.

Dumarest flung himself at the knife.

It lay where it had fallen, where Yalung had casually tossed it, the spot to which Dumarest had rolled after the Kha'tung fighter had pushed him. He reached it, scooped it up, sprang to his feet as Yalung realized his error.

"You fool," he said, already on his feet. "Do you think to beat me with that toy?"

Toy or not, the knife was the only advantage Dumarest had. He held it in his left hand, not trusting his right, holding it ready to throw. Yalung sneered at his indecision.

"Throw it," he invited. "Or use it to stab at me as you did before. Hurry and let us dispense with this farce. You are defeated before you can begin."

He crouched, thick arms folded over the massive muscles of his chest and stomach, complete protection to vital organs against a thrown blade. His chin lowered to shield his throat and his slanted eyes were watchful.

Dumarest studied him, knowing that he had only the one chance and that he had to make it count. He raised his hand and swept it forward in quick pretense. Yalung skipped backwards, hands lifting to beat aside the thrown knife, grunting as he recognized the feint.

A second time he took the same evasive action. The third his backward skip carried him to where the dead girl lay on the grass. His foot hit the obstruction and he staggered, off-balance and exposing his throat.

The knife ripped into the flesh below his ear.

It was a shallow cut but it was enough. Blood fountained in a scarlet stream, raining on the yellow and black, the grass, the body of the dead girl. Yalung clapped his hand to the wound, the fingers immediately turning red, more red spurting from the severed artery. He stooped, snatched up the knife, and threw it all in one quick movement. The point slammed against Dumarest's chest, tearing through the plastic to be halted by the protective mesh beneath.

"Armored!" Yalung swayed, already weak from the loss of blood. "I should have aimed for the face." He slumped to his knees and fell sideways, but he was not yet dead.

Dumarest walked to where he lay. A gleam of gold gave the position of the ring. He picked it up and slipped it on his finger, watched all the time by the slanted almonds of Yalung's eyes.

"The ring," he said, and raised himself on one elbow. "The secret, what—" He broke off as a thin, shrilling note echoed over the trees, the entire region. It was sweet, high and painful in its keening poignancy. "Look!" Yalung reared upwards to rest on his heels. "The ring!"

On the flat surface of the stone shone fifteen points of brilliance.

"A sonic trigger," gasped the Kha'tung fighter. "The correct sequence of the affinity twin. And you didn't know. You didn't know!" He fell, lips twisted in an ironic smile. "All I had to do was to kill you and take the ring. I had a dozen opportunities but I used none of them. I even saved you from the beast on Joy. I thought you were valuable, that you would have known that—"

He died as a second chime rang through the air. The summons to the guardians which announced the coming of a vessel to the Place.

The handler was an old man with silvered hair and lines meshed thickly on his face. He stood at the foot of the ramp, his eyes misted with gentleness.

"This job doesn't pay much," he said. "But it has its compensations."

"The pilgrims?" Dumarest looked at the column filing down the avenue. Their progress was slow, those who could not walk being carried by those barely able to hobble. Leading them was the enigmatic figure of a guardian. Others stood between the sparing trees. Watching? Counting? It was impossible to know.

"I was one of them once," said the handler. "Twenty years ago. I had a malignancy of the blood impossible to cure. Shrine was my last hope." He breathed deeply, inflating his chest. "I was cured," he said quietly. "It seems to me that I owe something to all those seeking health."

"It's a nice thought," said Dumarest.

"You crashed, you say?"

"That's right."

"You were lucky," said the handler. "And did you—?"

"Yes," said Dumarest quickly. "I visited the Place. And," he added slowly. "I think I gained what I had been lacking."

Gained and lost, both within the span of hours. From where he stood Dumarest could see the spot where they had slept, where Lallia had been murdered and where Yalung had died. The bodies were gone, lifted away by the birds to be disposed of somewhere, perhaps fed to the spine-trees. As others would be disposed of, those who would die, as some must die, at the center of the clearing.

He looked again down the avenue. The dying sun threw a ruby light in the natural arch, a dim, mysterious, luminescence in which the slowly moving band of pilgrims appeared to be walking through water, marching into the gate of another world. A concentration of pain and suffering, of desperation and hopefulness. Did the entity within the wrecked vessel live on such paraphysical emanations? Did it need the psychic energy of those who came to rest their hands on the mound? Giving, perhaps as a by-product, something in return?

"They go," mused the handler. "They crawl and skip and drag themselves down to the Place. And when they come back, those that do, they march like men. They fall into the ship and sleep solid for ten, twelve hours. Sometimes longer. And when they wake you can see paradise in their eyes."

"A good feeling," said Dumarest.

"The best." The handler sucked in his breath as a cone

of coruscating brilliance leaped from the surrounding area. "It won't be long now."

His face was livid in the glow. Dumarest turned, looking at the radiance, wondering what it could be. The discharge of natural energies? A waste product of the alien entity? Or was it, perhaps, the visible by-product of a supralight message aimed at some distant galaxy?

"They'll be coming back soon," said the handler. "And we'll take them home."

"And me?" Dumarest looked at the man. "You can give me passage?"

"If you can pay."

"To outside the Web?"

"To Thermyle; you can get an outward-bound ship from there." The handler hesitated. "We won't be going direct and you know the system. But if you're short of money you can ride Low."

"I've got money," said Dumarest.

He had Yalung's pouch of precious gems and they would carry him to where he wanted to go. To a flaring red point on a pictured galaxy or as near as he could get to the sector in which it was held. It would be a long journey and there would be too much time to remember what might have been. Of a girl with lustrous black tresses, the pressure of her arms, the promise of her body, the future they would now never share.

"That's all right then," said the handler. "Just you?"

"Yes."

"Then you're alone?"

"Yes," said Dumarest bleakly. "I'm alone."

**If you would like a complete list of Arrow books
please send a postcard to
P.O. Box 29, Douglas, Isle of Man, Great Britain.**

Other Arrow Books of interest:

IN OUR HANDS, THE STARS

Harry Harrison

When his test bench at Tel Aviv University unaccountably disintegrates, Arnie Klein knows he is on to something big. Too big to leave in the hands of a nation perpetually at war.

But even in neutral Denmark, Arnie and his terrible secret become the focus for international espionage, blackmail and intimidation.

Will the Daleth effect be the key to the stars – or a potential weapon of mass destruction?

THE RUINS OF EARTH
Thomas M. Disch (editor)

Cities choked by killer smog. Freeways clogged with autojunk. Nature running down – societies in crisis.

Man is at last waking up to the terrible damage he is inflicting on his environment. The various routes to disaster have already been charted.

But the damage still goes on.

This collection of stories by leading science fiction writers – each committed to a human vision of society – attempts to take the ecological inquiry one stage further. To indicate *why* we are destroying our world – and what the possible consequences for us all may be.

TIME IN ECLIPSE

David Garnett

On the surface: Medieval armies squabble endlessly over the remains of habitable Earth.

Underground: Shifts of watchers scan the video screens and ensure that nothing endangers the status quo.

A stable world – until the android giants, clockwork pigmies and extinct elephants start to materialise . . .

JACK OF EAGLES

James Blish

Danny Caiden has always thought of himself as a normal guy: an ordinary young American with no special talents leading an ordinary, uneventful life.

Normal, that is, until he suddenly realises he can see into the future.

Before he knows it, Danny has developed a dozen more alarming powers, lost his job, run foul of the FBI – and found himself at the centre of a shattering psychic struggle for the future of humanity . . .

A CASE OF CONSCIENCE

James Blish

A trap for humanity?

The four-man team of scientists investigating Lithia are about to make their report.

Two are in favour of exploiting the planet's enormous mineral wealth – if necessary enslaving its gentle, industrious inhabitants in the process. One recommends non-interference.

The fourth is Father Ruiz-Sanchez, biologist and Jesuit priest. For him, Lithia is Paradise – a Paradise created by the Devil himself . . .

THE QUINCUNX OF TIME

James Blish

THE DIRAC TRANSMITTER: key to space – and time

The new communications device had one huge advantage over ultrawave or the faster-than-light ships that still took months to carry a message from Earth to the outlying worlds. Its transmissions could be picked up instantly, anywhere in the Universe.

With an expanding interstellar empire to administer, Captain Robert Weinbaum reckoned his job would become a whole lot easier.

Until the impossible happened. Someone started monitoring the Dirac transmissions – before they were made.

CITIES IN FLIGHT: his famous science fiction quartet

James Blish

THEY SHALL HAVE STARS

A.D. 2018 – the Cold Peace, worse even than the Cold War with bureaucratic regimes in Washington and Moscow indistinguishable in their passion for total repression. But in the West, a few dedicated individuals still struggle to find a way out of the trap of human history.

A LIFE FOR THE STARS

The world's natural resources have long been exhausted and city after city goes 'Okie' – lifts off the earth to earn its living among the stars.

EARTHMAN, COME HOME

When the cities left earth, they moved into a constantly changing environment. In a multi-cultural universe an iron hand was needed to impose order upon the spaceways.

A CLASH OF CYMBALS

Earth is finished as a galactic power. Now, from the heart of the Milky Way, come the first tentative strands of the Web of Hercules – the strange culture that is destined to be the next great civilization of the galaxy.

THE SEEDLING STARS

James Blish

Pantropy: total genetic engineering, capable of modifying the human body to the requirements of the alien world.

Ganymede – an icy waste and the site of the first colony.

Tellura – a jungle world peopled by a stubborn breed of tree-dwellers.

Hydrot – where human personality lives on in the form of minute, underwater organisms.

New races of Adapted Men swarm throughout the galaxy.

HEROVIT'S WORLD

Barry N. Malzberg

Herovit's World – a place of terror where alien forces struggle for power.

Kirk Poland is a man of action – a man from another dimension. It was he who created Mack Miller, survey-leader and superman, hero of the space opera.

In another guise, though, Poland is the writer, Jonathan Herovit. Who wants Herovit's world? Certainly not Poland. And maybe not even Herovit himself.

In the ruins of a man's mind, the battle for supremacy has begun.

'This is Kirk Poland. Get this straight from the outset: I AM TAKING OVER . . .'

CHRONICULES

D. G. Compton

A mysterious explosion, a haunting indefinable smell . . .

Sitting quietly by a Cornish creek, reading his favourite comic book, Roses Varco hears the bang, catches a trace of the odour – and understands nothing.

Which is hardly surprising, since Roses has just witnessed the death of a time-traveller lost in a limbo between worlds. Had he known the truth, it would have terrified him – for that traveller was himself.

THE CONTINUOUS
KATHERINE MORTENHOE

D. G. Compton

Katherine Mortenhoe is dying. Dying in a world where incurable disease has become so rare that its victims are objects of avid curiosity, mercilessly pursued by the media.

In desperation Katherine runs from her tormentors. But not quite far or fast enough.

Sleeping rough among the rejects of society she meets up with Roddie a friendly stranger, – *who just happens to have a television camera surgically implanted behind his eyes. . .*